Breaking His House Rules

Also by Kelly Barker

Novels

The Inner Temple

Even the Gods Fear It

Necromantia

Short Stories

The Barber

Apple Tree

Off the Hook

Served Cold

A Dog Is for Life

Breaking His House Rules

By Kelly Barker

Breaking His House Rules is a work of fiction. Names, characters and incidents are products of the author's imagination, or the author has used them fictitiously. Any resemblance to actual events or persons, living or dead, is entirely coincidental.

www.kellybarker.org

Dedicated to Carol Barker.

Chapter One

Wherever you lived, there was always that one house. A house, eerie and stunning in equal measure, sitting on an acre of land with a private graveyard, surrounded by stone walls and known only by rumours and out-right untruths. Today, to Molly's annoyance, that house in particular, was now hidden behind overgrown conifers and what was once perfectly shaped topiary hedges. When the weather was just right, she had often come here to this quiet, almost forgotten part of town to sketch this magnificent house. Not only was it her bestseller at craft fairs, whether she used Acrylic or Watercolour in between the lines, she knew in her heart this house was her ticket to becoming a full-time artist.

Molly crossed the unused, yet maintained, road to the ornate black and gold gate and looked down the cobblestone driveway, hoping to spot the groundskeeper, Bill. She had often asked him if she could come in to paint the house. His reply, as well as his green overalls, never changed. “Which part of private property don’t you understand?” Which was always followed by a soft chuckle. When she asked him who owned the house, his reply to that question was always the same as well. “That’s none of your beeswax.” Again, followed by a chuckle.

Perhaps he was working behind the house today, she thought. Although, that didn’t explain why he hadn’t reshaped the topiary or cut back the trees from the house yet. Did he still work here? She hoped so; she was fond of him.

With her head wedged between the bars of the gate, she looked around the perimeter of the property and then tried to see any signs of life through the bay windows. She sighed. “Why are your curtains always closed? Who are you?” she asked the unknown owner.

Of all the ridiculous rumours around town, the most believable one was that the owner of this house was an old lord. But what would cause a lord to close himself off from the world like this? Did he have any family? If not, then she at least had one thing in common with him. Was he a recluse, or perhaps needed a wheelchair? That said, other rumours suggested this house was the lord's holiday home, and that it was only in use for a few days of the year. Which wouldn’t be too far-fetched in this town. *Oh... how the other half lived.* Even though Molly couldn’t afford her rent and bills without selling her art on the side, she’d never begrudged the wealthy. Instead, they piqued her curiosity, akin to watching documentaries about people with alternative views and lifestyles.

"Hmm, perhaps you keep your curtains closed to protect your art from the sunlight."

"Something like that."

Molly un-wedged her head from between bars and spun around. "June, you made me jump."

In her usual black and white attire, she laughed behind the back of her hand. "Are you doing more snooping than painting again? Actually, I'm glad you're here. I have a proposal for you."

Although the housekeeper was always pleasant, she was as elusive as Bill. Not that it detoured Molly's relentless questions. One of these days, June was bound to let something slip.

"Why hasn't Bill hacked back that green mass covering my view yet? I have a craft fair coming up soon. Oh, and I know Bill always says I'm not allowed, but if I could come in to paint the back of the house, I won't get in anyone's way." She tucked a lock of hair behind her ear. "Wait. Did you say you had a proposal? For me?"

"Yes, I did. The *green mass* ruining your view is yet to be cut because Bill has hurt his back—slipped a vertebra, and I'm looking for someone who can take over my duties while I look after him—"

"Why do you have to look after him?"

"You are so nosy, my dear." Her smile lit up her kind eyes. "Bill is my husband. So I don't *have* to look after him, I want to. Anyway, like I said, I'm looking for someone to take over my duties. Bill's doctor told him to rest his back before surgery, but since I'm approaching retirement, there will be a permanent position for you if or when he recovers."

"You and Bill are married? I didn't know that. So, that's the proposal? You're offering me the job?" She pointed to the house. "In there?"

The list of pros and cons for Molly's current job was huge, and yet there was only one pro: discounted art supplies. A combination of not wanting to leave work crying every other day because her manager was an evil witch and her desperation to not only see what was behind the gate, but to see what was behind those curtains, prompted her split second consideration.

"Well?" June said. "What do you think?"

"What's the pay like?" She un-tucked the lock behind her ear, then re-tucked it. "I only ask because my rent is so high."

"Don't worry, it's a perfectly good question. The pay is double the living wage—"

"Double?"

June's eyes lit up once more. "There are other benefits too. But, my dear, if you took the position, you wouldn't have to worry about paying rent. Accommodation within the grounds comes included."

"Is that optional?" She had lived in many foster homes, never feeling like she belonged. The flat, although she would never own it, was the closest thing she had to call hers. That being said, thanks to certain circumstances, she was now trying to find somewhere else to rent.

June shook her head. "You would be required to move in."

"Do you and Bill live here?"

"Yes, Bill and I have lived many happy years here in a cottage down from the main house."

Molly moved her curiosity to the side so she could focus on the negatives. What if she ended the contract on her flat, then found that she hated the job? What if the owner was difficult to work for, or hated her?

As if reading her thoughts, June said, "There would be a one-month trial, of course. In case you don't like it or you're not suited for the position. Although, I understand your concern if you hand in your notice for your current job, only to find out you don't like it here."

"It is a worry of mine." She frowned. "What sort of things would I be doing? Cooking, cleaning, changing the bedpan?"

June looked amused. "Other than a spot of cleaning, you will help the owner with his accounts, answering the phone, schedule meetings, and replying to emails."

Her face reddened. "I'm sorry. I just assumed he was... old. Retired, I meant. That's if being a lord counts as a job."

"Well, he's definitely old." She rolled in her lips to conceal a smirk. "And no, being a lord does not count as a job."

"So, he is a lord, then?"

"I simply agreed with your statement, my dear."

Something in the back of Molly's mind told her to run. Although, these days, since she'd learned life lessons the hard way, was she not always overthinking things and telling herself to run? Yet, this situation felt different. She didn't know June well, but she seemed trustworthy. And her perception of people, although jaded, wasn't completely off. Perhaps her mind wasn't telling her to run in the opposite direction, after all. Maybe it was telling her to run through the gate and to take the job? A job that could solve her current problems, answer her questions, and allow her to sketch any angle of the house whenever she wanted. Then the saying 'too good to be true' came to mind. A saying that had always proved accurate where she was concerned.

She looked over at the closed curtains. "Hmm. And the owner doesn't mind who you employ? By the way, what's his name?"

June held her head high. "The owner trusts my judgement, and the owner doesn't have a name until you sign a non-disclosure agreement."

Now Molly knew for certain which direction her mind was telling her to run to. She thanked June for considering her, then politely declined her offer.

* * *

The following day, Molly's eyes watered the second she stepped into the high-street. She stood and looked at the sign above the door of where she worked, like she always did, to compose herself. As she traced her eyes around the paint-palette and brush logo, her chin trembled. If she didn't work there, where else would she work? The art shop didn't just sell supplies, it had connections within the art community, and Molly wouldn't have sold half of her paintings if it were not for that. Even though she handed out business cards with her web address on, people preferred to pop into the shop to speak to her before commissioning her work.

She inhaled for five seconds, then exhaled. "I can do this."

"Do what?" said Molly's manager, Jackie. She continued to walk past, then stopped to face her. "I said, do what?"

"Nothing." She fiddled with her waist-length plait.

Jackie's nose scrunched up. "What was that? I didn't hear you."

"It doesn't matter." And that was exactly how Jackie made her feel: like she was nothing and didn't matter. Why she disliked her from the moment they met, she would never know. She'd never been late, never questioned her, and had always followed the rules sanctioned by head office. Perhaps that's what it was—nobody liked a goodie two shoes. Well, until recently, that may have been the case. Thanks to something she had no control over, Jackie now had an excuse for her scorn.

"You're a strange girl. Hurry, then. We have a big delivery coming in this morning."

Molly just nodded, then forced her feet to move forward.

* * *

Time moves slower in hell than it did in the living's world, or so Molly had read in a book. The author must have had first-hand experience, because her description couldn't have been more accurate. She looked at the clock again and wondered if the batteries had run out—even though she could see the minute hand working its way round. Ten more minutes until lunch.

"Come on, come on," she chanted.

Just as she hung the last of the fine brushes on the display stand, Jackie came around the aisle.

"Your boyfriend is here again. How many times do I have to tell you to leave your drama at home?" she said, standing in Molly's personal space.

She stepped back and then stepped from one foot to the other. "He's not my boyfriend. I told you, he won't leave me alone."

Jackie looked at her with disgust. "I don't care. He's your problem. Deal with it, and make sure he's gone before I come back from my break."

"But it's my break in a few minutes," she said, as she watched Jackie storm off.

When he tapped the back of her shoulder, she flinched before turning around. "Please, James." Her voice trembled, and she hated herself for it. "Not here."

His sneer was cruel, and he looked her up and down in a way that suggested he wanted to fuck her and hurt her at the same time. A look that even the best actors in the world could never pull off. A look that made her feel violated.

"I'm just here to see my favourite girl," he said.

Her eyes watered for the fourth time today. “Please, go. I can’t give you any money. I’m short this month myself.”

“I’m not here for money, you little bitch.” James got right in her face.

He always got aggressive like this when she guessed his intent. After only one month of dating, she knew he was bad news and broke it off, believing it would rid him from her life. That was six months ago. *How much longer will I have to put up with this? Why won’t he just get bored with her and target someone else?* Although, she wouldn’t want her worst enemy to experience this.

“Then why are you here?” More tears sprung from her eyes as she looked around at the customers in the shop, knowing she was about to be humiliated in front of them.

“I’m here because you called me.”

“No, I didn’t. You know I didn’t. Why are you here?”

“I need money and you’re going to give me some!” he whispered, then loudly, he said, “You owe me money and I need it back. I have bills to pay.” He didn’t have bills to pay, and he did things like that to make it appear as if she was the villain. That was why she had never called the police in the past. She knew they’d never believe her, or at the very best, they’d think they were as bad as each other and not do anything to help her.

Molly looked over the aisle at a customer shaking her head. “You… you said you weren't here for money, and I don't owe you anything. It's you that owes me, but I said you could keep it."

James owed her more than the four-hundred pounds he'd *borrowed.* In that one month they were getting to know each other, he'd eaten her out of house and home, broke her TV—which was yet to be replaced because she couldn't afford a new one. He had refused to get off her sofa one morning, leaving her with no choice but to give him her only key, which she then had to pay for a locksmith because he claimed he had lost it. Knowing now what he is capable of, she believed he said he lost the key thinking she had a spare one, making it possible for him to enter her home whenever he wished.

He tried to put his hands around her waist. "Come here."

This time, Molly found her voice. "Don't touch me." She backed away, looking around the shop. It was empty now—not that anyone would have helped her.

He noticed too and grabbed her plait, pulling her towards him like he has done in the past.

"*Get off.*" She snatched it back. When the staffroom door opened, and Jackie marched out, Molly's surroundings became a blur, making her feel like she was having an out-of-body experience.

"What the hell is going on?" Jackie said.

Before she could answer, James said, "She asked me to come because she said she had my money. I don't know why she's acting like this." His confusion appeared believable.

"No." she turned to Jackie. "I swear, I didn't."

Jackie shook her head. "You can't play games like this, especially at work. And you,"—she turned to James—"why do you keep falling for it."

Molly spoke before James could tell her more lies. "No, Jackie. It's not like that. I've changed my phone number so he can't ring me, and I don't have his. I swear."

As if she had never said a word, they continued to speak as if she weren't there. Tears streaming down her cheeks found their way into her jumper while she listened to James telling Jackie that he was worried for her, and that the heart wants what the heart wants. Jackie went from being angry to looking at him with sympathy in her eyes.

However, amid the pain she felt in that moment, there was hope—something she hadn't had before now. It was a house in the forgotten part of town where June and Bill lived, who had been nothing but lovely to her. A place that came with accommodation if she took the job. Which meant she wouldn't have to put up with her neighbours giving her dirty looks in the communal hallway because James was trying to get into her flat by buzzing on their doorbells at all hours. She would have a fresh start by disappearing for a while. And if she hated the job, with double the living wage and no bills, she could save up and move to Scotland, Wales or wherever the hell she wanted. She looked at Jackie and spoke before thinking about the cons. "I quit."

They continued to speak as if she wasn't there, and because James was a master-manipulator, they now spoke as if they were good friends.

"I said, I quit." Although adrenaline caused her voice to tremor, she felt relief and a smidge of power wash over her.

Jackie glanced at her then back to him. "James, it would be best if you go on your way."

His smile looked genuine. "You're probably right. I'll see you around, Jackie." As he was walking away, he said, "Molly, you can pay me back whenever, but don't phone me again unless you have it, okay? Maybe you should speak to a professional and get the help that you need."

She returned his fake smile with one of her own.

When he left, Jackie turned to Molly. Her top lip was curled up in disgust. "You quit, do you? You know, you shouldn't say such things. Or I might actually believe it and find someone to replace you."

"We've had a job vacancy sign on the door for ten months. Good luck running the shop by yourself." Molly left her stuttering while she walked to the staffroom to collect her things.

As she was leaving, Jackie stepped into her space. Never again. "Move out of my way."

"If you do this, without handing in your notice, you won't get a reference from me."

"Where I'm going, I don't need a reference." She hoped. Just as she thought Jackie wouldn't move, someone walked through the door, forcing them both to play nice.

The customer looked to Jackie for help, giving Molly the green-light to walk out the door without looking back. She walked around town twice to make sure James wasn't lying in wait so he could follow her, then ran towards the house.

Chapter Two

Out of breath and on the cusp of an anxiety attack, Molly searched for a doorbell or something to announce she was here. How did June get in yesterday? She ran to the stone pillar to the left of the gate. There was a keypad lock for the double gates, but nothing more. She rubbed her heart as thoughts of June requesting a reference or telling her the job had gone took her from the cusp to a full-blown anxiety attack. That smidge of power she felt earlier today mocked her. What had she done? How would she pay her bills now? She ran to the other pillar, knowing it doubled as a letter and parcel box. There had to be some sort of communication device. What if something needed to be signed for?

"There," she said, as she pressed a small button under the brass letterbox. Static crackled from three grooves above the opening, so she spoke into them and hoped someone would hear her. "Hi. Hello."

"Is that Molly?"

"It is. Hi, June. Can we—" The gate's mechanics clanked to life as the right-hand side opened inward.

Assuming that was her cue to enter, she crossed the boundary, then stepped to the left so the gate could shut. When it did, the sound of the lock snapping into place rang out and lingered in the air. A new fear joined her existing one, fuelling her anxiety levels even higher.

For many years, she had stood near to where she was now, eager to be granted access. Would she feel disappointed by what she discovered? Would she fall in love with her surroundings, only to experience further heartbreak if June decided she wasn't suited for the job? She cursed her ex for showing up today, putting her in this position. Would he always cause her misery?

Molly looked over her shoulder to the gate—she couldn't turn back now, even if it was open.

The sound of June's heels on the cobblestone driveway snapped her back into the present moment, and her friendly face quelled her trepidation.

"Are you okay, my dear? You look distressed."

Molly couldn't feel her feet on the ground as she walked up the drive-way, meeting her halfway. "Hi. Umm, is the job still available?"

"It is. Shall we talk over a cup of tea first?" The concern in June's eyes and tone almost broke Molly. It wasn't often someone cared enough to show her that level of compassion.

Unable to talk in fear of crying, she just nodded.

"Follow me. I'll take you to mine and Bill's home first, then I'll take you on a tour." She said as she passed through the stone archway connected to the house.

Molly's eyes widened. "The house is much bigger than I thought. It's a mansion"

"I suppose it does look quite small from the front."

No, it didn't. It was still an impressive size. As they neared the back, not only did Molly note that all the curtains were closed, she spotted something coming into view over the state roof. "That's a spire—a tower. No, what are they called?"

"Are you referring to the turret? There were four originally. When the house got renovated, before my time, the owner had one from the back and the front two removed. Since we no longer live in mediaeval times, or need to defend our homes with bow and arrows, he didn't want the upkeep."

"Or more windows than necessary," she said under her breath. "Why did he keep one?" Molly stood below the remaining one and looked up, then over the back of the building—which now looked more like a castle than a house.

"That one is the library, and was his mother's favourite room in the house before she passed away. The owner can be sentimental."

June's words went a long way to calming her nerves. Thoughts of the owner being a mean old lord now seemed a little harsh. Although, him being sweet-natured didn't come to mind, either. The lord, if he was in fact one, drifted from her mind as she traced her eyes over the stonework and the ivy. She stepped back so she could take more in, and to see which angle made the house more flattering.

"You'll have plenty of opportunities to paint it if you take the position, and perhaps you'd prefer to do it from further back."

Molly frowned, then turned to June. However, her eyes didn't make it to her—not even close. What she saw was surreal, almost magical. "Wow. Bill is great at his job, isn't he? He's an artist, too."

"He is, and he takes a lot of pride in making it not only aesthetically pleasing to the eye, but a haven for the wildlife as well. Follow me, you'll have plenty of time to investigate."

Molly looked around and couldn't guess which direction they were headed. "Where's your home?"

"We're just down from the treeline," she said, as she made her way to another stone archway.

Once they walked through it, the graveyard she'd only ever seen from a distance, and after the trees had lost their leaves, came into view and took her breath away. Even more remarkable, was a large lake behind it. And although the skies were grey today, it sparkled, and she couldn't believe she never knew of its existence. She felt her shoulders slump after the tension from earlier left her. Being this close to the headstones, complete intricate carvings and Bill's green fingered creativity, made it seem so tranquil—a place of reflection more so than loss.

"This place is stunning. So peaceful. Does the owner spend a lot of time out here?"

"The owner no longer leaves the house, not even to spend time in his gardens." She said it like one would announce what day of the week it was, and yet, Molly sensed a hint of sadness in her tone.

Perhaps the owner was in poor health. If so, did that mean he would soon die? What would happen to his staff if he did? She hated to overthink things, but in this case, her soon-to-be livelihood was on the line. "Why doesn't he leave the house?"

"We're here." Across a beautifully manicured lawn sat a picturesque cottage. "This is where we live. I forgot to mention something yesterday. Your accommodation will be within the main house. The entire top floor to yourself. Not that you need all that space, but you'll feel a sense of much needed privacy." She opened her door without unlocking it. But then, who would know this cottage existed?

She was about to ask why she had the top floor, and thought it would also confirm her suspicion of the owner needing a wheelchair, when she heard Bill call out.

"Is that little Miss Nosy? I'm afraid I can't get up. Well, I can but—"

"Stay put, Bill." She motioned for Molly to enter the living room. "Make yourself at home while I put the kettle on."

"Okay." When she saw Bill, she felt a little relieved. He didn't look to be in too much pain. "How are you?"

"The pain medication is doing its job. Put it that way." He said, followed by a chuckle. "It's all a part of getting old, I'm afraid. Well, unless you're a vampire."

Molly cocked her head to the side. "I'm glad the meds are working. I just walked through your handiwork. You're amazing at what you do."

There was a momentary flash of pain in his eyes when he shifted to get more comfortable. Meaning, he wasn't completely under the influence of the meds. "That's thanks to my little helpers. If you help them out, they'll help you in return."

Or maybe he was. "Umm. Helpers? Oh, the bees. You're talking about the bees."

He laughed. "You didn't think I was talking about the garden gnomes, did you? No, those little terrors keep hiding my tools."

Molly put her hand over her mouth, not knowing how to react.

"I'm just teasing you. The medication might make me drowsy, but they don't give me the power to see things that aren't there."

She laughed. "I'm sorry. I wasn't sure."

June walked in with a tray and Molly's stomach rumbled when she saw the assortment of biscuits. "Have as many as you want, my dear. You, Bill, can only have two."

"Two? The doctor didn't say I couldn't have biscuits." His tone was teasing, and Molly felt foolish for not noticing it earlier.

"I know she didn't, but now that you're not as active as you usually are, they're bad for your health."

She put four on his saucer next to his tea before handing it to him. “Right then, Molly, let’s discuss the position in depth. Are you able to start right away, or do you need to hand in your notice?”

Molly flushed. She hadn’t expected her to ask that question, and didn’t want to start this new chapter with deceit. “I have to be honest. I quit today. Umm, my manager can be… difficult and I couldn’t take it anymore, and walked out knowing I had a second option. But, I would understand if you didn’t want to employ me now because you think I’m irresponsible. I’m not by the way. Umm…”

June's expression gave nothing away. “First, that’s your manager's loss. It’s clear to me you’re not an irresponsible person. Second, ‘umm’ is not a word the owner tolerates. I’m afraid you’ll be leaving a ‘difficult’ manager behind, only to be replaced with another one. As is life, my dear. But the benefits are worth it, and he’s not so bad once you get to know him.”

Molly looked over at Bill to see if he agreed with her statement. “He’s a good-en—deep down. He just likes things done in a certain way, and he doesn’t like change. Including the way the English language is evolving.”

“And he dislikes swearing.” June added. “And nail biting. I see your nervous tick is to fiddle with your hair. He can’t complain about that.”

Molly dropped her plait. “Thank you for still considering me for the position. But he sounds strict. What if he doesn't like me?”

"He is, and he isn't strict. If you make a mistake, he'll say, mistakes happen. If you keep making the same mistake over and over, he'll speak to you about it and offer you help. And although he may snap, he never raises his voice beyond that. Also, what's not to like?" She sipped her tea with a hint of a smile in place.

"He sounds fair." She concluded his pickiness came with his age, and if she didn't accept him for that, then it would be ageist. Her customer service was great, and she decided she would use her charm if need be.

June smiled. "That he is. You seemed distressed earlier. Was that because you walked out of your job?"

Actually, it was mostly because of what James had done, forcing her in this position, but that was almost behind her now. Her fresh start was about to begin and she didn't want it tainted by saying his name aloud. "It was, and I was worried that the job offer may no longer be available."

"I'm glad you're okay now. I just have some forms for you to look through and sign, then I'll show you around, and then—more importantly—where you'll be staying."

"Forms? You mean the non-disclosure agreement?"

"Don't look so worried. Although, I'm quite certain you wouldn't believe what you may or may not discover, and neither would anyone else even if you were to break the agreement." She looked as if butter wouldn't melt in her mouth before her lips curved into a grin.

Bill tutted at June, then looked at Molly. "She's just teasing you. You'll forget all about the non-disclosure agreement when you're doing what you really love doing in your spare time."

Unfortunately, his encouraging words didn't have the desired effect because little did they know, she'd just walked away from one situation where no one believed her and now she was being forced into another.

* * *

The interior, from what she could see, was more modern than she expected, and she was pleased to see that the owner liked art. His black framed paintings had a white inner border frame, complimenting any colour, and yet still in keeping with the decor—which was also black and white. If only she could admire them fully.

"Why are all the curtains closed? I understand the owner wants to protect his artwork, but there are some windows that can let in the light without direct sunlight touching them."

"The owner isn't a fan of sunlight." June continued to walk into what she assumed was the main living space. "Do you recognise the one above the fireplace? Wait, I'll turn the lights on."

When she did, about twenty or more lights flicked on. Every piece had its own picture light. When she finally saw the piece above the fireplace, she put her hands over her mouth. It couldn't be. It was. "That's one of mine, of this house. One of my winter editions."

"And the owner's favourite. The fact of where it's placed is proof." June looked fondly at it.

"But, how? I would have known if he purchased this from me. I know this address by heart." She searched her mind, trying to remember the faces who had bought from her at craft fairs. When she couldn't picture an elderly gentleman, it was beside the point because she remembered he never left the house.

"You haven't gone unnoticed by the owner. He asked me what I knew about you, and I told him you were an artist—which was apparent, and where you sold your artwork. I found your website after you told me about it. Then the owner chose a piece, and I had it sent to the post office first before it got delivered here. Our privacy is imperative, as you will soon find out."

"This is amazing. Unbelievable. I remember leaving it at the post office because I was worried about it, and I went back the next day to make sure someone picked it up." She shook her head. "Isn't it time I knew his name? It seems rude now to just refer to him as the owner."

June didn't hide her amusement. "The owner doesn't have a name until you officially start working for him."

Molly smiled—and why not? Things were looking up for her.

"Shall I show you to your rooms?"

She followed June through a different hallway to the one they came through and found herself at the bottom of a double staircase. As she walked up, she was delighted to see more framed art along the way. Not only was visiting art galleries her favourite pastime and her escape from the world, she was about to live in one.

This time, when June entered the room, she opened the curtains. The walls were white and the trim and soft furnishes were black.

"There isn't much furniture up here, so you can either bring your own, or we can have some moved up from the guest room. Not that we have any guests. You will also be more than welcome to decorate how you wish. However, something tells me you will appreciate the white walls when you hang up your own artwork."

She was right. Molly couldn't paint her—whatever colour it was supposed to be—walls white, because her landlord wouldn't allow it. "I wouldn't change a thing." She looked around. "This room is bigger than my entire flat."

"It can be your bedroom, workspace or anything you want it to be." June walked over to a door on the other side of the room. "This is your main bathroom."

Molly let out a steady breath before she followed June, then entered. "Oh, my goodness, I have seen nothing like this before."

Unlike the rest of the house, light streamed through the skylight. The black claw-foot tub looked magnificent against the white marble, and the large, black framed church mirrors gave the room an otherworldly feel. However, it was the many exotic plants that had her eyes widened in disbelief. Some were taller than her and some hung from the metal frame of the skylight.

"It's more like an indoor greenhouse than a bathroom." She walked into the centre and turned twice to take it all in. "It will feel like I'm in a jungle when I have a bath and the steam fills the room."

June looked pleased. "Bill will never put a healthy plant down. When the upstairs became no longer in use, he moved them all in here. While he's resting, you wouldn't mind taking care of them, would you?"

"Of course I wouldn't mind. It's a shame that the owner can no longer enjoy this room. If you don't mind me asking? What's wrong with him? Medically, I mean."

June shrugged. "Other than sometimes being an old-fashioned grouch, he's perfectly healthy."

Chapter Three

June could have organised a removal van for the following day, but Molly wanted an extra day to pack, take things she no longer needed to the charity shop and to have a day to herself to let everything sink in. While she was packing away her art books, a sense of excitement sparked within her. A good omen, she thought. Even if she was walking into the unknown. Although the excitement perhaps wasn't for her new job, it was her new canvas. If the front of the house was her bestseller, just wait until people saw her paintings of the gardens and the interior. She may have lost a few customers by leaving the art supply shop, but she was about to have zero money concerns. She could take her time creating her latest collection before releasing them to the public. Word of mouth from her new customers would reach the ears of her existing ones.

"Are you ready with the last box?" the removal van driver asked from the communal hallway.

"I am." Molly hadn't smiled this much since… ever. She stood at her front door to say goodbye to her old life, and although she would wait until her one-month trial was over before ending her contract on the flat, she hoped to never see it again anytime soon. And so what if the owner was too stern, or didn't like her? She would take it on the chin and win him over.

* * *

Shortly after Molly put the last of her clothes in her new walk-in-wardrobe, which was bigger than her old living room, she heard a light tap on the door. She straightened her clothes, un-tucked and re-tucked her hair behind her ear, then prepared herself to meet the owner. Should she thank him for buying one of her pieces? No, not yet. She would let him do the talking. Her hands shook when she turned the handle.

"Breathe," she told herself. When she opened the door, she didn't come face to face with the ageing owner, or anyone. "Hmm."

Sitting upon a side table in the hallway, was a vase filled with a beautifully arranged bouquet and some paperwork. After she closed her door and found the perfect place for her bouquet, she sat on her sofa to read the card that accompanied the flowers and a letter. The first was from June and Bill, congratulating her on her new role, and reminding her that if she needed anything, to let them know. She breathed out a content sigh and felt she couldn't feel luckier even if she lived a thousand more years.

The second seemed as if someone had typed it on a typewriter, and the paper itself was something she had never seen before. Her heart quickened and quickened, more so after the second and the third time she read it.

House rules:

- **Do not open curtains during the day, unless you are within your living quarters.**
- **Do not invite guests into the house or on the grounds.**
- **Do not enter the ground floor after dark until the following morning.**
- **Do not enter the library—under any circumstances.**
- **Do not enter the basement—under any circumstances.**

Breaking the rules will result in the termination of employment with immediate effect.

Regards,
Theodore Ardelean

* * *

The following morning, Molly was in the downstairs office with June while she was showing her which emails to respond to and which to bin.

"Your primary job is to confirm orders, take payment, and then organise the delivery."

"Why can't I open the curtains if he's not around?"

"Because the owner—Theodore doesn't want them open. At the moment, all the patrons are regulars. You'll soon get to know all of their addresses by heart." June's eyes were smiling.

"And why can't I go into the library or the basement? What if there's a book in there I want to read? Or what if I wanted to put a bottle of wine down there?"

"You, my dear, can buy your own books, and since when have you been a collector of wine? Now, other than this, you'll do a spot of cleaning on this level of the house and pick up his dry cleaning."

"If I can't open the curtains, how will I see what I'm doing when I'm cleaning?"

"Lights, my dear. You'll turn the lights on." June stood, then motioned for her to sit in the chair. "Do you have any questions?"

Molly laughed while she sat. "Other than work related stuff, would you answer them if I asked?"

June pulled out the chair opposite the desk. "No, I wouldn't. Perhaps you'll find the answers to your *many* questions in time—when the time is right. You are highly curious, and with that level of curiosity comes open-mindedness. Something you will need while living and working here."

"You realise you're creating even more questions, don't you?"

"Ask me what you're taking payments for. That should scratch an itch." She leaned over the desk to retrieve her tea.

It's not as if Molly wasn't curious about that, but taking payments for unknown items and organising deliveries was hardly as peculiar as the house rules. "Okay, what exactly am I taking payments for?"

"Blood," she said. "Theodore runs the largest blood donation organisation in the world."

She grabbed her plait with both hands. "So, people donate their blood, and he sells it. That's wrong." Could she really work for someone who did that? Be a part of an organisation that fooled people into thinking they were doing a good thing? No, she couldn't. Not for all the money in the world.

"No, my dear. He doesn't sell the blood, but organising deliveries doesn't come without cost. For example, if the UK wanted to donate blood to a country in need of it, we provide storage with thermal insulation inserts and various configurations of frozen or chilled coolant packs are used to maintain temperature, which is adjusted, depending on the duration of the flight. Then there are air crafts and fuel to think about, and thousands of staff members worldwide in zero contamination factories, making the storage. That's what people are paying for." She seemed a little put out, and Molly felt guilty for it.

"I'm so sorry. I, umm, well…"

"It's okay. It's a good show of character, to question things that don't appear sincere. That being said, you'll soon come to realise Theodore is an honest vam—person, and is always working on new ways to keep the cost down for those who need blood, and then there is his staff and their wages to think about. It's a juggling act I don't envy."

Molly couldn't help but look around the spacious office, complete with Persian rugs and heavily lined velvet curtains. Even the crystals dangling from the chandelier proved their authenticity by emitting rainbows over the ceiling. For the first time, she felt as others do where the wealthy are concerned, because making a profit from charities and basic human needs was where she drew the line.

"I know what you're thinking," June said. "First, this is his family home, maintained with family money, and he donates the surplus. Second, he has never lorded his wealth over others. Like my Bill said, he's a good-en. A stubborn, surly good-en."

She stuttered before she found her words. "I'm sorry. Er, I… This world is new to me. I have no right to judge anyone."

June came around the desk to put her arm around her shoulders. "Don't worry, you didn't know. You can find all the information about the organisation in those folders behind you, in case you wanted to see for yourself. Actually, it's quite interesting and I'm proud to be a part of it."

"Yeah, I think I will be, too." She frowned. "I didn't think to ask until you mentioned family money, but does the owner have children?"

"No, not yet, but there's always time."

"Umm, if he hasn't had children by now, he might not be… able to." Obviously, a man can have children at any age—if he can still get it up, but she couldn't imagine the ageing lord being a first time dad. "Has he ever been married? Oh, I forgot to ask. Is he a lord?"

June laughed. "That's better—I have my Molly back. I have to get back to Bill, so I will only answer one of your questions. Which one will it be?"

She grinned. "The second one."

"Technically, he is, however, he no longer wants to use that title." She clapped her hands together. "Right then, I'll leave you to it. Theodore's dry cleaning needs to be picked up by this afternoon—take a couple of hours to yourself while you're out. And I will come back to cover you, which isn't always necessary, but a kitchen fitter is coming by to take measurements for a new cooker. Use the phone if you need me, or if you need to see a friendly face, you know where we live."

She wanted to ask why there wasn't a cooker in the first place, but June had already turned to leave the room.

* * *

Molly synced the laptop to her mobile, enabling her to be aware of incoming emails, and then took her time to appreciate the rest of his art collection before lunch. She would have to have toast again, and felt thankful she hadn't donated her toaster before she moved in. "But why would you have a fridge and cupboard full of food if you don't have a cooker?" she wondered aloud.

There was a kettle in the kitchen, though, although something told her only June used it for when she worked in the house. She made her way to it to make herself a coffee. Maybe the owner—Theodore—had his own cooker in his kitchen downstairs, in the basement, she thought, as she pulled her mug from a cupboard. That had to be the case because before June arrived this morning, Molly had looked in every room, except the library, and concluded the owner's bedroom and living quarters were down there. Still, it didn't explain why his food would be up here if his kitchen was elsewhere. Or why he would choose to sleep in the basement. Was he allergic to sunlight? No, because surely June would have mentioned it when she said other than him being an old-fashioned grouch, he was perfectly healthy. Or she would have mentioned it to make her understand the importance of why the curtains must remain closed.

While the kettle was boiling, she leaned her back against the worktop, and looked up at the ceiling to admire the intricate coving.

"What the..."

Was that a camera or an alarm? There wasn't a red light, but then, the newer ones didn't have them, did they? She walked out of the kitchen, down the hallways, through the rooms, then in all the rooms upstairs, only to discover that there was one, sometimes two, in every room.

Her hand had been on the library door handle this morning, and she had turned it only to find it locked. She had thought that if it had not been, how would he have known whether she had peeked inside. *Just a quick look wouldn't hurt,* she would have told herself. Now she was grateful she couldn't get in. Wanting to know how close she would have been to losing her job if the door was unlocked, she went back downstairs and saw that there was a camera facing the library.

She wanted to ask June about it, and she would, but first she wanted to see if she could justify it. Wherever you worked, there were cameras, in fact, even just walking through town was now caught on camera. And when she heard people complain about them, she always said to herself that they were there to keep you safe, and that you shouldn't worry about them unless you were doing something you shouldn't be doing. However, no one knew who it was who was behind the cameras watching you throughout town. Here, she did know, and it put her on edge.

"It's a small price to pay," she said, trying to convince herself it was fine. She subconsciously put her hand over her mouth, wondering if he could hear her too, then she reached into her pocket for her phone to call June.

While Molly was on the way back with the dry cleaning, her mind felt chaotic with racing thoughts. First, she felt conflicted about being in town this soon after leaving her old world behind. She needed to get out of the house—which wasn't a good sign, and she didn't want to be seen by anyone she knew. James or Jackie. Second, she kept relaying the conversation she had with June about the cameras. She had simply laughed it off and had said they were just there for security and nothing more, and that Theodore wouldn't have the time to watch her around the house as if she were a goldfish in a bowl. When she asked June why going in the library was against the rules if the door was locked, her reply, after she laughed at her again, was that it didn't surprise her that she had tried to open the door.

Anyway, what was the alternative? It's not like she would leave because there were cameras in every room—that would surely be an overreaction. So, she would have to let that anxiety go. After all, there were only so many concerns a person could deal with before they lost their mind, and she refused to have a sleepless night over it. Also, if the owner *was* spying on her, then she could spy on him too. While she walked, she unzipped the hanger bag to investigate his clothes, then stopped and giggled.

"Black, silk shirts? Very sexy, Mr Ardelean." She shook her head then hurriedly zipped the bag back up before she got to the gate.

Just as she'd seen June do many times before, she used the code given to her when she moved in to unlock the gate and enter the property. Then there was a different code to the front door, to which she felt lucky because it spared her the worry of losing the key.

June hadn't told Molly what to do with the clothes once she returned, so she headed to the kitchen to see if she was still here, but before she made it that far, she saw movement down the hallway. Her heart pounded until she realised who it must be.

"Are you looking for the loo? It's actually this way." He appeared to not have heard her when he continued to walk away, so she hurried towards him. "Excuse me."

When the kitchen fitter turned, he rendered her speechless. Never had she seen a man so handsome. He appeared to be older than her, but no older than thirty-five, with his thick, black hair swept back from his vibrant blue eyes. She could also smell his masculine scent from where she was standing—which wasn't close enough.

"May I… umm, I'm sure June has already offered, but… umm, would you like a drink? Talking of me making you a drink, you were looking for the loo, weren't you? You'll probably want to do that first before you have another. That's if you've already had one, that is. Er, it's this way." She turned to hide her reddened cheeks, motioned him to follow her, and then was reminded why she could never have a decent boyfriend. Because who would want a blithering idiot to call theirs?

When she realised he wasn't following her, she doubled back to him. "It's this…" Why did he look so perplexed and irate, she wondered. "... way."

He took two strides in her direction, and if he wasn't over a foot taller than her, they'd be nose to nose. "'Umm' and 'er' are not words." Not only did the kitchen fitter have an Eastern-European accent, it dripped with authority. His eyes narrowed and the colour of them flared even brighter.

Realisation hit her so fast, she was yet again rendered speechless. Not that she'd know what to say if she could. When she rubbed her free hand over her heart, in a futile attempt to prevent it from exploding out of her chest, he stepped back, and she let out a steady breath.

He took another step back. "I see you are back early with my dry cleaning. June told you to take a couple of hours off before collecting them. Why didn't you listen?"

Because she didn't want to be in town any longer than she needed to be. "I… Er."

He raised his brow, then held out his hand.

Not knowing what else to do, she shook it. When he didn't squeeze her hand back, and gave the hanger bag a pointed stare, she felt embarrassment to the likes of which she had never experienced before.

"Oh, you were reaching for your clothes. Yes, of course." She dropped the bag. "I'm sorry."

Molly was about to retrieve them when he beat her to it. He straightened, slowly, and his eyes were penetrating, making her turn away.

"I'm sorry," she repeated.

"June is in the kitchen with the *kitchen fitter*. You may as well choose which cooker you want now you're back."

When Molly sensed him walk away, she looked up, wanting to thank him, but she couldn't find the words. Then she watched him turn the corner toward the basement door.

Chapter Four

Theodore slammed his door closed and cursed June for employing the artist. Why her? Of all the people. Why did she have to choose her? But then, he knew why June had done it, didn't he? He let out a steady breath. She had done it for him.

He walked through the dark hallways to a room emitting the only light source in the basement, which came from the many computer and monitor screens arranged on his large desk. Before he looked at one screen in particular, he momentarily prepared himself by rubbing his hands down his face, then he whipped them away when he caught a whiff of her scent on the hand she had shaken.

The screen showed him the artist still standing in the hallway, in the same spot where he left her, with bewilderment etched into her perfectly formed heart-shaped face. He had already clocked that her nervous tick was for her to reach for her plait, like a comfort blanket, and the fact she was yet too, told him just how shocked and obviously confused she must be feeling. After all, she had thought he was a senior citizen. A belief he wanted her to continue to have until he convinced June to find a replacement. But was that what he really wanted? Yes. No. He groaned.

How unprepared he was to be seen by her, and let alone this soon. But then, hadn't he always fantasised about having her hazel eyes focused on him, then of him undoing the plait she always wore, only to know what her pale-brown hair felt like when he ran his hands through it? To run his tongue over her sun kissed skin, then taste her. He shook his head to dislodge the thought, then asked himself if, on some level, he wanted to get caught? No, of course not, it was too dangerous. So why did he go upstairs to ask June a question he already knew the answer to? Why take the risk? He didn't want to admit the answer to himself. Out of habit, Theodore's eyes flicked to the screen which recorded the front of the house from the gate, which pointed to the spot where Molly had often sat to paint his home. No need to do that now, he told himself, because he now knew where she was at all times—even more so than before.

He had hacked into the town's high street surveillance many years ago, when it first got installed, and had barely watched more than a few minutes of it. Then, a couple of years back, Molly began painting his home, and looking for her amongst the cattle became his obsession. When he successfully convinced himself he did it out of boredom and nothing more, he went a step further.

The town's surveillance cameras, by law, could not operate in residential areas. However, thanks to the scaremongering tactics used in today's marketing, almost all homeowners owned a *hackable* doorbell camera. And there was a house across the road from Molly's block of flats that had the latest model—thanks to him sending them an upgrade anonymously through the post.

He'd watched her comings and goings daily. Watched her brace herself before she walked to walk, brace herself again before she entered her place of employment, and then watched her cry while she walked home. It took tremendous strength to do what she did every day, and although it hurt his heart to watch her cry, he felt proud of her too, and silently cheered her on. And he knew, from seven-hundred years of life experience, her dreams of becoming a full-time artist were within reach, not only because she was exceptional, but because her talent was intertwined with sheer determination. She was a force to be reckoned with, and she didn't even realise it. Perhaps if it wasn't for those fuckers in her life and the fact she didn't have a supportive network of friends and family, she would have.

Her reasons for not having a supportive network were her own, and he had never pried into her past. Although, it would seem she was too busy working towards her goals to socialise and didn't have a family, which told him she was a runaway, or possibly in foster care rather than being adopted.

He swept a gaze over his desk at the four-by-six framed photograph of his own adopted daughter, June. He could kill her for doing this to him, even if her heart was in the right place. She knew he was more than content just watching Molly's routine inch closer and closer to her dreams because he had told her many times. But then, that had changed when that *boy* walked into her life, hadn't it?

When Theodore saw him enter her home and not leave until the following morning, he had smashed all his screens up in a fit of unexpected, and unfamiliar to him, rage. Jealousy was a new emotion to him, and he didn't want to feel it again, so he didn't replace his screens for over a month. When he did, he vowed he wouldn't look for her. But old habits are hard to shake and shortly after he installed the new monitors, the vow broke. However, he didn't find what he expected—which was her enjoying the honeymoon period of her new relationship. Instead, he saw her fiddling with her plait and glancing over her shoulder while she walked home from work. It didn't take long for him to conclude the boyfriend was the cause of her upset. Theodore felt his canines biting into his lower lip. Even if he had the desire to leave his home, there was no justification for killing humans, not these days, anyway. Not to mention it was against the law. His law. Although, for some humans, there were exceptions.

In any case, Molly was out of reach from her dickhead of an ex now. So, perhaps he wouldn't urge June to get rid of her after all. Or had he already decided from the beginning he had no intention of doing so? Possibly. When he tried to convince himself that she would be safer within his home than out there, he laughed without humour. No, she wouldn't be, but he'd make it safe for her by staying out of her way. No more risks. Especially not now, after she had expressed attraction towards him.

With his head resting on his hand, he squeezed his eyes shut, picturing the way her jaw dropped and her eyes softened when he turned, and how she breathed out a sigh of appreciation before she stumbled over her words. And then there was her scent, something he wouldn't allow himself to think about if he was to stay away from her. But no matter how strong willed you thought you were, when you tried to not think about something in particular, your mind rebelled against you. So he cursed himself when he recalled how her scent had made more than his canines extend—hence the anger he felt with himself and the swift exit he made. The remorse he felt, knowing she believed his anger had been directed at her, made him feel conflicted. It served a purpose in keeping her away, and yet his instinct wanted her to want him. He brought the hand she shook to his nose, then he again whipped it away and shook his head to dislodge the thought of her. This time, he would not break his vow. He couldn't. Not if he wanted to keep her here.

As soon as Molly put one foot in front of the other, Theodore used his keyboard to switch from one camera shot to another. She was heading towards the kitchen, so he switched on the listening device built into the fake air vent.

At first, he heard June talking to the kitchen fitter about nothing in particular, then she said, "Molly, my dear, you look like you've seen a ghost."

She frowned. "It's a possibility. That's if the old owner died, and then reverted to his youth in the afterlife."

Theodore smiled despite the situation he found himself in. Watching her was one thing, but listening to how she spoke and interacted with people created a whole new level of excitement he could do without but couldn't turn his back on. His finger wavered over the button to turn off the sound, unable to make himself press it.

The kitchen fitter looked from June to Molly, clearly eager to see where this conversation was headed, then landed on June, most likely because her eyes flared with mischief before answering. "And did this youthful ghost tell you off for not using proper words?"

She put her hand on her hip. "Yes, he told me off. I thought he was an old man."

The kitchen fitter chuckled. "This house is a mystery, that's for sure. And the reason I always clear my schedule for you, June."

Molly looked as if she'd only just noticed him. "I'm so sorry. Hi."

"Hi, to you too. It's a pleasure to meet you." He tipped his imaginary hat, then slid a catalogue across the worktop towards her. "I'm told this cooker is for you. Would you like to choose one? I can pick it up from the manufacturers myself whenever you're ready, so there's no rush."

"May I have this one, please?" She pointed to the one on the cover, then looked at June. "You told me he was… I thought he was… a lot older."

June blinked, feigning innocence. "Whatever gave you that idea?"

The kitchen fitter looked amused. "I'll leave you ladies to it, and I will be back tomorrow afternoon to install the cooker."

"Many thanks for stopping by at short notice. I'll show you to the door."

After Molly thanked him and said goodbye, she immediately sagged when they left the room, then as if she sensed someone watching her, she straightened to look up and into the camera.

When their eyes met through the screen, Theodore inched closer, and ran his tongue on the inside of his fangs. "Enough," he said, then turned off the monitor.

He would not give in to temptation. But then, if he didn't see and hear her, wouldn't that make him want her more? He switched them back on, no longer recognising the male he had become. He was the most respected vampire in the world, only second to the royal family—the only royal family his kind recognised as legitimate—and now he was reduced to this. If his kind discovered he was obsessing over a human, he wanted to do more with than feed from, he'd be the subject of ridicule. That being said, his beloved mother had been born human. Father like son, he supposed, then smiled fondly. He could only imagine what his father would say to him now, and he would sell his soul to hear him encourage him to take Molly as his bride. Yet, the world had changed so drastically since his father's death. In the last hundred years, the world had developed at such a phenomenal speed; it left Theodore feeling as if he had experienced time travel. Sure, he marvelled at the latest tech, but it was the way the humans had developed which caused concern.

No longer were they believers of the supernatural, or even the occult, for that matter. Instead, they worshipped science and dismissed anything unexplainable. Not that he was unexplainable, but when the vampire population was only three million compared to the eight billion humans who populated the world, it would mean the end of his race as they knew it. Why? Because humans feared what they couldn't explain. And there was only one way they'd want to conduct their experiments; which would be to have a live specimen under a microscope, and in restraints.

He shivered when buried memories of Marcus resurfaced. The young vampire had revealed himself to the humans and allowed them to study him. Little did he know—after cutting his finger off to show them how it regenerated—that they would keep cutting his arms and legs off so he couldn't escape. When Marcus was finally located in the late nineteen-twenties, all that remained of him was his head, torso, deranged mind and three female sires created from his blood. According to the records they found, over two thousand men needlessly lost their lives in the attempt to create vampires before the so-called scientists concluded only females could survive the transition; and that was only if they were in exceptionally good health.

The high council, which Theodore was a member of, had ordered the destruction of the facility, the surrounding towns, and all the records. They dispatched assassins to dispose of the scientists, their family members and associates. Marcus and his sires, after all attempts to bring them back from madness failed, were put to death. It was a hard lesson for all of them, and one they would remember for eternity.

That being said, many of his brethren had infiltrated the TV, film and literary industry, in a desperate bid to turn the tide and make humans more susceptible to them, and so far, it was working—slowly. But they would never reveal themselves; it was merely a safety net. A safety net they needed because of the inability to foresee the future caused by how fast the world moved forward. Although, there were a handful of humans that knew of their existence; they were called the Omniscient (all knowing) and had to be approved by the high council beforehand.

Theodore supposed that's why his affections for Molly were harder to bear than it needed to be; not only would she survive the transition, the council would accept her because he'd make sure of it. However, he would not turn her life upside down, or for her to experience the pain of transition.

When he looked back at the monitor, Molly was still by herself, which meant June must have left. He shook his head and picked up his phone to see what she was playing at.

She answered on the second ring. "Yes, Father."

"Don't use that innocent tone with me. I have never fallen for it."

She laughed. "Go back upstairs and get to know her. In the normal way, opposed to the stalker way."

Theodore counted to three before answering. "I have repeatedly told you, it is too dangerous. She has her whole life ahead of her."

"And I have repeatedly told you that Bill and I will not live forever. The thought of you being alone after we pass away keeps me awake at night, and I want to enjoy my retirement, and not spend it worrying about you." June's voice quivered towards the end.

He let out a steady breath, unable to bear her upset, and he could never stay angry at her, knowing his time with her was short. Had she not been born with a genetic heart condition, he would have offered her immortality at twenty-five. The council believed humans were at their healthiest at that age, and therefore, it became law that they couldn't transition until then or once they've passed that age.

"I won't be alone. I have…"

"No one," June finished. "Anyhow, you must have known on some level she'd be a part of your life. Why else would you completely renovate the house to make it look like an art gallery?"

His daughter knew him so well. And she was right; other than his associates, he didn't have anyone. Head back in hand, he sighed.

She continued. "She's here now, and it *is* what you wanted. Whether you can admit that to yourself. Just get to know her. Let her get to know you, and then let her decide." She paused. "Father, I have to go. I need to make Bill some food so he can eat something before taking his medication."

"Of course. Have a good evening," he said.

"You too. Bye."

After he hung up, he looked at his screen and saw that Molly had left the kitchen.

"Where are you?" He clicked away at the keyboard to find out, and when he found her, he grinned. She was standing outside the basement door with her ear pressed against it.

Chapter Five

Molly couldn't hear anything beyond the door. She eyed the keypad lock to the left and wondered if perhaps it was the same code used for the gate or front door. But even if it was, what then? Just walk down there and introduce herself? Not likely. Plus, it was one of his rules. And there was no need for another introduction after they'd already met. The thought of it reddened her cheeks all over again. Although, why should she be the one to feel embarrassed? People shook hands all the time when they met and didn't he like things done the proper way? Or did he just pick what he deemed was the proper way to suit himself? Most likely, she concluded.

Then her mind went where she really didn't want it to go. She tried to wipe it away by reminding herself how rude he was, only for it to reappear with his mouth-watering appearance, his eyes, lips, jaw, hair, and his height. Everything about him was perfect. It's as if he was made especially for her.

"Oh, shit." Was that butterflies she felt? That was proof, she decided. Proof she was attracted to, or attracted arseholes. But was he really an arsehole? June and Bill didn't seem to think so. And weren't people a little more critical of their employers?

Molly rewound her mind back to the conversations she'd had with June and what she already knew, hoping to see things from his point of view. He didn't leave his home; not even to visit his gardens. The curtains had to remain closed, but she'd already decided he wasn't allergic to the sun. So, what else? Did he suffer from agoraphobia? So extreme that he didn't even want to see the outside world? Possibly. She had wondered why he had closed himself off from the world before she started. But then, she had assumed he was at least seventy-plus years of age, and she couldn't have been more wrong. She frowned when she remembered June confirming her statement, by saying he was definitely old. However, knowing June that little more than before, perhaps she was referring to his temperament; old before his time.

"An old soul," she said, then looked around his modern home. She shook her head. "No, not quite." Or perhaps he was just keeping up appearances on this level of his home, and the basement was a more accurate reflection of his personality. But even if he had agoraphobia and was an old soul, that didn't explain why being downstairs after dark was off limits or why she couldn't have guests?

Perhaps he disliked people, hence why he never went outside or wanted people inside?

"But if that was the case, why choose an organisation that helped people?" Or, more likely, he could just be socially awkward, because he worked from home and wasn't surrounded by people, or he shut himself away because he'd always been like that. She'd have to ask June about that one, and then remembered she already had this morning, only for June to say she'd find out when the time was right. Either way, she decided she would give him the benefit of the doubt.

Her phone pinged; notifying her she'd received an email. A flutter of anxiety beat throughout her chest. June had shown her how to reply, take payment and organise deliveries, but now that she knew lives were on the line, she had the added pressure of not messing this up.

When she sat at the desk, she opened the email and saw an order form before her for ninety blood bags to be delivered within the United Kingdom. She then opened up another program, which automatically calculated the price after you applied the order and location. It seemed low, so she double checked again, and again.

"Nope. That is right." It still seemed strange, though. Why would someone want blood bags delivered to what seemed like an average home address? Surely they should be sent to a hospital first? She shook her head, replied with the receipt, then remembered that June had said it was okay to send the shipment before payment because people and charities always paid in their own time. And why wouldn't they? She supposed it was because they couldn't order more if they didn't. She pressed send.

"So, that's it? Easy." Pleased with herself for doing something she hadn't done before, she headed towards the kitchen to make herself some food to take upstairs. There wasn't a set time when she was supposed to finish, but the sky was darkening and the rules stated she went upstairs. Also, where had the time gone? No longer was she in hell, begging time to move faster. Still, she would take the laptop up with her too. Her new job was straightforward, with each order taking only minutes to complete, so why not do a bit of overtime? Maybe it will even earn her some brownie points? And even though she could have died of embarrassment when she met the owner, she let out a sigh of appreciation when she realised for the first time in a long time, she wouldn't be crying after work while she walked home.

* * *

Molly was in the black claw-foot tub with her hair pulled up into a messy bun, marvelling at how fast tension left her body. She'd never had a bath before, well, not in her adult life; her flat didn't have one. And as predicted, she felt like she was in the middle of a jungle within the steam and exotic plant filled bathroom, and never had she felt so relaxed; especially after she stretched her pink ankle-socks over the cameras in her rooms. That said, there wasn't one in the bathroom, anyway. She'd searched everywhere, including behind the potted plants. So, if Theodore was watching her, at least he wasn't a complete peeping Tom.

She giggled, closed her eyes, then went under the water, imagining how it might piss him off to find the screens of his monitors coloured pick. Except, that's not all that came to mind when she thought of him, it was the shade of his eyes, surrounded by thick, black lashes, and she could tell, while in his black shirt, that he was lean, possibly muscular. Her fingers traced over her breast, past her stomach, to between her legs.

Then she came up for air. "No, no, no." She would not allow herself to have a crush on her boss. "He was…"

He was what? She had decided to give him a chance, which meant she had no defences against him now. Oh, well. It's not like she had plans to pursue anything, anyway—even if he wasn't her boss. She was, well, her, and because of the way James had treated her, she had sworn off all men. So fantasising about a man she could never have wouldn't hurt her, would it? When her fingers traced back between her legs, she didn't remove them until she was satisfied.

* * *

"Why does he have an Eastern European accent?"

"My dear, I have only just walked through the door. Say good morning first, then ask me if I want a cup of tea." June had entered through the back, which led straight into the kitchen. She took her coat off and hung it by the door.

"I'm sorry. Good morning. Would you like a cup of tea? By the way, why does he have an Eastern European accent?" Molly flipped the kettle on.

She snorted. "Stop apologising for everything—even if you were just being sarcastic. Just so you know, Theodore rang me earlier to tell me you worked until late last night."

Molly's mind raced. Had she not covered all the cameras? "How did he know?"

June frowned before opening the fridge to retrieve the milk. "It states the time on the email when it's received and replied to." Then she smiled when she understood where Molly was coming from and looked up at the camera. "They can make even the most innocent of people feel paranoid, can't they?" Yet, they are everywhere you go now."

"Except bathrooms."

"I can't imagine there's much to steal from a bathroom. Not unless the thief likes fancy towels," June said casually, pulling out two mugs from the cupboard.

"So, they are just for security?"

Then she opened the drawer and took out a spoon. "That's why security cameras were created. Are you making this tea or am I?"

Molly stifled a laugh. "You're very secretive, to the point where you wouldn't crack under pressure in the interrogation room—even if you were having your toenails ripped off."

She tried not to laugh while she poured hot water into the mugs. "And you are lucky a cat has nine lives, quarters were on. Not unless… "Can you switch the cameras on and off in my room with this surveillance program? What I mean is, can you choose which sections of the house you want to see?"

She pulled the keyboard closer to her and tapped away. "There are twenty-nine working cameras in and around the property, and if you count, you'll see the same number of angles on the screen at once if you click back to the main menu. Here, I'll show what it looks like when you turn a camera off."

Molly edged forward. "It's just a blank screen. So if they were working cameras in my room, and they were off, would they just show me blank screens?"

"Correct. Like I said before, there are cameras everywhere these days, but most, I suspect, are fake or turned off. However, they are still effective. Similar to non-working speeding cameras slowing cars down. I'll tell Theodore you want yours removed."

"No, it's fine. Especially now that I know they don't work. I wouldn't want him to think I'm complaining."

"He wouldn't, but so what if he does? This is your living and working space too. We want you to feel comfortable."

Molly sighed a sigh of relief.

June squeezed her hand. "Other than meeting Theodore and feeling like you're being spied on, you are enjoying it here so far, aren't you? No regrets?"

She squeezed her hand back. "I wasn't happy where I worked, and I cried most days I was there. And last night, I wasn't awake all night worrying about the next day, and I didn't wake up this morning feeling sick with dread. Am I enjoying the job? I don't know yet. But I woke up early and enjoyed every minute of it while having a coffee in Bill's garden before work."

"In this weather?" She feigned shock before smiling. "I'm sorry you had a hard time where you used to work, and I'm pleased to hear you're enjoying elements of the job."

"Oh, you mentioned this morning about me taking late night orders. Should I not have, or…" She trailed off so June could fill the rest in.

"He just wanted me to tell you there was no need because he covers the orders after hours. Think about it like this; you work days, he does the night shift."

"Okay." Molly nodded. "Is that why I'm not allowed on this level after dark? Because he likes to work alone."

June stood and stepped away from the desk with the two empty mugs. "My dear, I have to get back to Bill, so I only have time to answer one of your questions. Didn't you want to know why he has an accent?"

She laughed in her hands and shook her head. "Oh, I don't know. Umm, does he like to work alone? No, no. I want to know why he has an accent."

"His parents were Romanian."

"Oh, okay. Interesting." Before, when she thought he was much older, it made sense to her he would have lost his parents. Now that she knew better, she asked, "Is his dad still around?"

"No. They both passed away—many years ago."

"He must have been young." Her own past threatened to resurface in her mind, so she pushed it back by asking another question. "How old was he when he moved from Romania? It couldn't have been long ago."

"That's another question for another time. Why don't you pop by for lunch? Since you've been without a cooker for a few days, I bet you'd appreciate a cooked meal."

"I would, thank you. I don't suppose you'd quickly tell me why there wasn't a cooker up here before I moved in?"

She shook her head with a hint of a smile. "I'll see you later today."

Molly's phone pinged. "See you soon."

It was another order, and she was thankful for it; her mind needed a break from her constant sleuthing. However, it would seem that she couldn't get Theodore out of her mind—no matter how distracted she was. She wondered if perhaps losing his parents was the reason he closed himself off from the world. And that perhaps he felt isolated and didn't move back to his place of birth because this house held fond memories for him. After all, June said he was sentimental.

She decided then that she would reach out to him. She looked at the landline and thought against it. June had given her his number in case she needed help with orders; not for a chitchat. Plus, she knew she'd panic and start blabbing. No, instead, she would write him a letter, explaining that she had a firsthand experience about losing both of her parents, and although their circumstances may differ, she understood how he must feel and that he could talk to her if he wanted, and then she would slip it under his door before she went to June and Bill's for lunch. But first, she had an extremely easy and stress-free job to get back to.

Chapter Six

Theodore hung the phone up with June and thought over what she had said about Molly, feeling uncomfortable about the cameras in her private rooms. So he opened a separate file which monitored the upstairs—a file he had separated from the rest of the cameras to remove temptation from watching her twenty-four-seven and give her privacy. However, before he permanently disabled the cameras, he saw that she'd covered them with something pink. He smiled at that and then saw movement from a different screen. His heart picked up its pace when he watched her slip an envelope under his door.

After he retrieved it, he propped up against the headboard on his bed to read her letter.

Dear Theodore,

I wanted to thank you for my employment, accommodation and cooker. It also flattered me to see you had purchased my art. Thank you for your support.

Your house is my bestseller, and I'm itching to paint the back—that's if it's okay with you?

I'm also writing to tell you I lost my parents in a collision when I was seven. The roads were wet when they swerved out of the way of an oncoming car in the wrong lane, then their car flipped before hitting a wall. My grandparents told me they had died at the scene and probably thought it would help me with the grieving process if I knew they hadn't suffered. But it doesn't matter how you lose your parents, it's painful either way, especially when you're told you're going into foster care shortly after. To this day, I cannot forgive my grandparents for not taking me in. I don't know if that makes me a bad person, but I cannot move past it.

Anyway, the reason behind this letter is to let you know I'm here if you want to talk to someone about your loss, even if our experiences are different.

Best wishes, Molly

* * *

As soon as Molly slipped the envelope under his door, she regretted it. The feeling intensified when she looked over at the graveyard on her way to June's cottage, and berated herself for not remembering he already had someone to talk to. And who better than June? Would he think she was brash for sticking her nose where it didn't belong? Had she really over stepped this time? She remembered and held onto the words June had said to her earlier today, and they and therefore, can afford to be overly curious. You're clearly and understandably uncomfortable about the cameras, so after these, I'll show how you can access the footage from the cameras on the laptop. That should quell your inner detective for no more than five minutes."

Her eyes widened. "Really?"

June nodded. "Yes. And if you think Theodore is spying on you during the day, you can get him back by spying on him during the night."

"Are there cameras in the basement? Will I be able to see what's down there? See him down there?"

"I don't know. I've never looked." She shrugged.

Why would she not? Wait. "Do you think I'm overreacting? Or crossing a line?"

She looked affectionately towards Molly before handing her a mug. "You're simply more inquisitive than me, and it's probably because you are new to this house, whereas, I'm not. You must never stop asking your questions or being who you are, do you understand?"

Kindness was still new to her, and it made her feel emotional. So all Molly could muster was a nod.

* * *

June was right: having access to the footage only quelled her inner detective for less than five minutes. She was disappointed she couldn't see into the basement, but it also pleased her to discover that none of the shots showed her anything but pink socks. Meaning, that none of the cameras in her living brought down her anxiety—but only by a smidge. Anyway, she had done it now and couldn't take it back; she told herself, then stopped walking, taking in deep breaths to further calm her nerves. When that didn't work as well as she wanted, she carried on until she was at June and Bill's front door. She rang the doorbell, then heard him call out, "It's open."

She reached for her hair and stepped from side to side, not knowing what to do. Finally, the door opened and Molly was pleased to see June—even if she was grinning.

"Why are you still standing out here?"

"I'm sorry. I have never just let myself in anywhere before."

June widened the door even more so she could pass. "Stop apologising for everything. I said you're always welcome and our door is always open. Just let yourself in. Theodore does. Well, he used to."

Molly filed away that statement for another time. "Okay. Thank you."

They entered the living room, and she took the same seat she had before. "Hi, Bill. How's your back?"

"It's as good as it can be." When he shifted in his chair, pain etched in his face this time. "My doctor booked me in for surgery next week, and then after that, I'll be on bed rest for another six-months."

"Something tells me you're not so fussed about that, but not being able to look after the gardens is going to be hard for you."

He nodded. “It will be, but June tells me you’ve been enjoying this morning, and that's enough to lift my heart a bit.”

“I will paint them this afternoon, too. I can’t wait to get started.”

He beamed and June said, “I’ll set the dining room table. I made lasagne. Is that okay with you?”

“Yeah, that sounds lovely.”

Molly saw affection in Bill's eyes as he watched June walk out of the room. Then he looked back at her, grinning. “I hear you met the *old* lord yesterday. He’s a fright when he doesn’t smile, isn’t he? Actually, what am I saying? He's more of a fright when he *does* smile. But you'll get used to his teeth.”

She laughed at his joke—even though she didn’t get it—and felt comfortable enough to tell him about her experience.

“And he didn’t shake your hand?” Bill tutted. “He knows better than that. I’ll tell him off the next time I see him.”

“It’s okay. I did assume he was the kitchen fitter and tried to give him directions in his own home.”

He laughed at that, then said, “I would have liked to have been a fly on the wall. That said, always remember you’re safe and he would never intentionally upset you. He’s just curt, whereas you are not. A personality clash you can live with, am I right?”

It wasn’t like Molly hadn’t dealt with worse. “You're right. I thought perhaps that he didn’t like people, and that’s why he doesn’t leave the house, but that assumption conflicts with his organisation. An organisation that must have saved thousands of lives."

"By now, the organisation would have saved millions, if not more. Theodore doesn't dislike people, but he feels as though the world has left him behind, and in some ways, it has, and he no longer feels a sense of belonging. Even though you're young, you must have noticed how quickly the world moves on."

"Yeah, I have noticed, and it's scary. Do you think him losing his parents played a role in that?"

Bill cocked his head, as if trying to remember. "I wouldn't know. His parents died long before I was born, and his dismissal of the world occurred about twenty years ago."

Molly frowned, then smiled when she remembered he was on strong medication. "You mean before you started here? Maths isn't my forte, but that would make Theodore a hundred years old at the very least if they died before you were born?"

"Lunch is ready," June called from the dining room. "Bill, do you need me to pull you up and out of that chair?"

"No, I'm not feeling too stiff today," he called back and shifted to the side before standing, then to Molly he said, "It was nice to take a break from those tablets today—they block me up."

Her mouth fell open at his honesty before she followed him into the dining room. Then they sat down and talked about everything and nothing at the same time while she ate the best lasagne she'd ever tasted. Before Molly left, June gave her the rest of the lasagne in a tupperware container to reheat and eat later because she was still without a cooker. The entire experience, from the moment she walked through the door to making her way back to the main house, seemed surreal to her because she had never felt so welcome. And she felt proud of herself for not feeling bitterness towards her past for missing out on what most people took for granted. Instead, she filed it in her good memory bank.

* * *

After she found the perfect spot, she set about sketching the outline of the turret, set behind a willow tree, which was set behind Bill's artistically manicured garden, on her blank canvas secured to an easel. However, she couldn't give her new project her full attention because she kept weaving in and out of her meditative state to think about what Bill had said. If he hadn't taken medication today, why would he say something so impossibly impossible? Perhaps the medication still lingered in the mind for hours after taking them. She nodded in agreement with herself, then put the end of the pencil in her mouth and nibbled the top. But then, as she got to know him a little better over lunch, she learned he was as sharp as June was. Still, mistakes happen. And yet she found herself glancing over her shoulder at the graveyard where Theodore's parents were most likely buried. Carved into the marble would be the dates of their deaths, and would prove to her whether or not Bill was under the influence. Then she wondered what that would mean if

Bill wasn't mistaken, then smiled at her own wild imagination.

What if June was spot on when she asked her yesterday if she'd seen a ghost? What if Theodore was a time traveller? If he was from the past, that would explain why he feels the world has moved on without him. What if he *was* allergic to the sun because he was a vampire? That would explain a lot.

She stepped towards the graveyard, then stopped. "I'm just being silly. That's all."

As she continued to sketch, today's events and regrets left her momentarily, reminding her why she loved doing what she did. Not only had it helped her dissolve past traumas, it was the source of her strength she used to get up every morning and keep going. She nibbled the top of her pencil again. Perhaps that's what was missing from Theodore's life; he needed more than just his organisation to run. Her thoughts of him had really taken a turn after learning more about him—which was nice for him, she supposed, but not so much for her if her feelings continued to grow stronger for a man she still barely knew and could never have even if she did.

Anyway, enough of that, she thought, and went back to her drawing, which was getting more difficult to do as the sky was darkening. She pushed on for as long as she could, then tutted when she could no longer see the outline of the willow tree. While she was packing away her equipment, light flashed in the corner of her eye. All the downstairs curtains opened simultaneously, as if they were on a timer, and the lights she left on in the house crept over Bill's garden. "Shit. Shit."

She took a couple of hurried steps towards the house, then stopped. Should she go back to Bill and June's cottage? Would he really end her employment if he caught her out after dark? Surely not. But she wouldn't take the risk. She was yet to end the contract on her flat, so it was not as if she had nowhere to go, but with no job, she couldn't pay the rent. Plus, she would lose her two new friends. As she was about to turn back to the cottage, she saw movement. It was him, walking from one room to another, as if he was searching for something. What could it be? She cupped a hand over her mouth. Was he making sure she had gone upstairs? She knew what she needed to do next, but she couldn't take her eyes off him.

He stopped, ran his hand through his hair, then looked out the window in her direction. He then left the room, entered the kitchen, and opened the back door.

Knowing it was too late to turn around now, her feet moved in front of the other against her will until she stood before him. "I, umm… I didn't realise how late it had gotten. I'm sorry."

He surprised her by leaning against the doorframe with his arms crossed over his chest. "You didn't realise the sun had gone down?"

Normally, such a question would have ignited her inner temper, but he had said it without a trace of condescension and had sounded more curious, if anything else. So she answered honestly. "I lose track of time and my surroundings when I'm sketching or painting."

He seemed to consider this, then said, "You'll have to set an alarm in the future. The rules are in place for a reason." He moved away from the doorframe so she could enter. When she didn't move forward, he raised his brow. "Are you going to stand out there all night? I think not."

"I, er… about that." she dropped her easel when she reached for her hair.

He stepped forward to retrieve it, and she noticed he crossed the threshold with ease.

"You are very clumsy." He picked it up and instead of handing it to her, he stepped back into the house with it and looked at her expectantly.

She didn't appreciate being called clumsy, especially since it couldn't be further from the truth. It was his fault for making her feel nervous. When she thought she had the nerve to correct him, she lost it when she stepped through the door and had to brush past his body because he hadn't moved back far enough.

"About the rules," she said. "When the moon is full, the landscape couldn't be more stunning, and I love to paint it. Also, what if I wanted to go out after dark to… socialise and stuff?"

He looked expressionless when he looked into her eyes and was yet to reply, which suited her just fine because she liked the view—until it became awkward.

"Umm."

With his free hand, he lifted it towards her face, un-tucked a lock of hair from behind her ear, then ran his fingers through it. “So soft.”

Instant arousal pooled within her, causing her to breathe in deeply. She felt her body temperature rise with an even mixture of desire and embarrassment before stepping back. “I’m sorry,” she said, annoyed with herself for apologising when it was him that should have said it. She looked at her feet.

“Don’t apologise. Look at me.” When she did, he continued. “I will amend the rules for you, Molly. Now, upstairs.”

How the hell had she found herself in a position where a man, who was not her father, was telling her to go upstairs as if she were a child? She rolled in her lips to conceal a smirk.

“Is something funny?” he asked. Again, with more curiosity than anything else in his tone.

She nodded her head, “No,” she said, then stifled a laugh. “I’m sorry… I mean, I’m not sorry. No. What I mean is; I didn’t mean to say sorry.” She put her hand over her mouth to shut herself up.

Unexpectedly, Theodore’s lips curved. “Upstairs, please.”

If Molly were honest, going upstairs right now, couldn't have come at a better time. She needed to decompress after another mortifying encounter with her boss. “Good night.”

“Good night, Molly.”

After casually walking out of the kitchen, she ran through the hallways and up the stairs. When she shut her door, she slid down it, then realised he hadn't mentioned the letter, and that he still had her easel.

* * *

The following morning, after another romantic bath for one and many inappropriate fantasies about the boss from the night before, Molly woke up surprisingly refreshed. She dressed in her best outfit and put on a little more lip gloss than usual, telling herself it wasn't for his benefit, and left her hair wavy and loose. When she opened the door, she came face to face with her easel and an envelope attached to it. Deciding she wanted privacy while she read it, she went back inside and sat on her sofa. Her hands trembled when she opened it.

House rules:

- **Do not open curtains during the day, unless you are within your living quarters.**
- **Do not invite guests into the house or on the grounds.**
- **Do not enter the ground floor after dark until the following morning—unless there is a full moon.**
- **Do not enter the library—under any circumstances.**
- **Do not enter the basement—under any circumstances.**

Breaking the rules will result in the termination of employment with immediate effect.

Best wishes,
Theodore Ardelean

She crushed the letter to her heart. Not only had he amended the rules, he wrote 'Best wishes', proving he had in fact read her letter. And if he were angry with her, surely he would have said something. After she read it one more time, she put it with the other one and made her way downstairs to make a coffee and do more sketching before she opened any emails.

* * *

Theodore watched Molly set up her easel in the garden from his screen, and wondered what she thought after seeing the amended rules. Was she pleased? Did she roll her eyes?

He had decided, after reading her letter and initially being unable to find her last night, that he would do what he could to keep her here by making her happy. Because when he couldn't see her on any of the inside cameras, and after he had rang and asked June if Molly was with her, only for June to say she wasn't, he felt a deep loss. An emotion he felt after losing his parents, and feels when he's reminded that June and Bill will not be around forever. It was then that he realised something he had known all along. Something he could no longer ignore. Obviously he couldn't have her in the way he really wanted—which was her beneath him, while she ran her hands down his back, but he would do the next best thing and keep her close to him. Which would mean no more tears after work and shitty boyfriends hurting her. He was protecting her; he had decided. “I’m just keeping her safe from the world that hasn’t been fair to her,” he said, mesmerised by how her hair swung with her movements.

Chapter Seven

Before Molly went outside to set up her equipment, she had heard movement coming from the kitchen. Her heart had quickened because it couldn't possibly have been June at that time of the morning. Before she had peeped around the corner, she ran her hands through her hair and straightened her already snuggly fit jumper, only to feel disappointment. Clearly, June had already been and gone.

"Hi. Did June offer you a drink?" she had asked the kitchen fitter.

"Hello. No, it was the young lad who let me in," he had said. "And yes, please. I would love a strong coffee."

Molly nodded, pulled out two mugs and flipped the kettle on, and cursed herself for missing him by minutes. Because who else could the young lad be?

"I would have been here sooner, but it turns out that the cooker on the cover of the catalogue is the most popular one and I had to wait an extra day for it."

"That's not a problem."

"They came shortly after I arrived, too." He tipped his head towards the kitchen's island.

It was not like Molly hadn't noticed the enormous bouquet of red roses, but in a house like this, weren't they expected? A wealthy person's version of an ornament? Or their version of an air freshener? Or both?

"Who are they for?" the kitchen fitter had asked, eager as she was to have some mysteries of this house answered.

"Oh, they're probably just for the house." She had handed a coffee to him. "For decoration."

"What does the message on the card say?"

She had frowned, walked around the island, and found it. "I don't know."

"Well, open it. If it's for the house, I'm sure it wouldn't mind if you read the card." He looked amused.

"You're right." She had placed the envelope in her pocket and told the kitchen fitter where she'd be if he needed her for anything.

Standing beside her easel and a garden chair she used as a makeshift side table for her coffee, she pulled the envelope out of her pocket to read it, then put it back. Apart from the flowers from June and Bill, congratulating her on her new job, she had never received a bouquet before. But what if they were just for the house, as she suspected, and the envelope just contained the receipt from the florist? She could already feel the disappointment seeping in her heart if they were not for her.

She pulled out her pencil, getting ready to add more detail into the garden, then stopped. Or what if they were for her, from him? Her hand reached for her pocket. But did she really want to receive roses from him, if they were in fact for her? She did, and she didn't as memories of James kissing her roughly, pulling her hair and trying to touch her body resurfaced, making her shudder. There was only one way she wanted to enjoy her employer, and that was in her mind—only. And yet she had been disappointed to find she had missed him by mere minutes this morning, and she had worn her hair down, admittedly, for him. So, trying to convince herself she only wanted an in-her-own-mind-relationship with him was futile. She sighed in defeat as she remembered the way he gently ran his fingers through her hair, with the look of affection in his eyes, and realised he was chipping away at the jaded wall she had built. She pulled out the envelope and opened it.

Consider this the handshake and welcome you should have received. T. A

Molly had to admit, as pleased as she was that they were for her, she felt conflicted. What else had she been expecting? Still, her roses were a lovely gift, and she would keep the card as a treasured memory.

"You're up early."

She jumped at June's voice, then giggled. "So are you. The kitchen fitter is here, and I made him a drink. Would you like me to make you one?"

"No, my dear. You're working." She stood in front of her easel. "I don't know how you do it. I really don't. It's as if you've taken a photo."

Molly blushed. "Thank you. It will look great when I add colour. And don't tell Bill, but it's for him, for when he gets back from the hospital."

Her heart sank when she saw a flash of distress in June's eyes before she smiled and said, "He'll be so pleased."

"Are you worried about his surgery?"

"No, he's a tough old boot. I'm worried that he won't be back to his usual self after the six months he's been told to rest."

"I don't know what to say. We could both chip in and help with the gardens, I suppose. Oh, I know, I could do the boring jobs like sweeping the patios, cutting the grass and raking up the leaves. It will free up more time for him to do what he really enjoys."

"You're an absolute sweetheart—never forget that." She picked up Molly's empty mug from her makeshift side table. "I'll make you another."

She smiled, went back to her project, then wondered which question she would ask next about Theodore. There were so many and she was thinking about writing a list, but for now, she would ask yesterday's question.

When she heard the back door open, she looked over the top of her easel. It was June with two mugs and a widespread grin on her face.

"The roses are beautiful. Did they come with a card?" She set the mugs down and pulled up another garden chair.

Molly nodded and handed it to her. "I saw him last night, too—after hours."

She quickly read it, then handed it back. "You did? And I bet he wasn't angry with you for breaking his stupid—except for one—list of rules."

"No, he wasn't, and he amended the rules for me." She tilted her head to the side. "Which one rule isn't stupid?"

"Hmm." She sipped her tea. "That's for me to know and for you to find out when the time is right."

Molly was about to ask why when June cut her off. "Yesterday, you wanted to know when Theodore moved from Romania and whether he preferred to work alone. How about I answer them both? Would you settle for that instead?"

Her eyes widened. "Yes!"

"He is a solitary creature—but then, they are by nature, so he's more than comfortable in his own company until he finds someone special to share his life with. And he never moved from Romania. You were right, he was born here."

Molly repeated her words over in her mind, trying to make sense of them. "That doesn't add up. If he was born here, he wouldn't have a foreign accent, and are you suggesting Romanians are solitary people? I've not travelled the world, but I know enough to know we're all the same. Oh, I know what you've done.

You've worded your answer to create even more questions."

June laughed with tea in her mouth, forcing her to spit it back into the mug. "Oh, look what you made me do. I'll have to make another. No, I wasn't suggesting that Romanians are solitary." She pointed to the house. "Theodore was born and raised in that house. His accent was inherited from his parents."

Her lips curved. "You don't inherit accents, June."

"You do if you're homeschooled, and taught how to speak in the parents native tongue before learning English."

Suddenly feeling inadequate, she rubbed her hand over her heart to soothe herself. "I didn't put two and two together and come up with him speaking two languages." He was the most attractive man she had ever seen, wealthy, and, of course, highly intelligent. *What* had she been thinking? Feeling embarrassment creep over her cheeks, she swept her hair over her shoulder so she could plait it.

"He speaks nine. But you, my dear, speak many languages as well." June stood up, put her hands over Molly's, then unravelled her plait. "You speak the languages of creativity, compassion, optimism, integrity and many others. What's this? Don't cry."

She sniffed. "I'm just not used to… this. I, umm…"

"I have to be honest with you. Yesterday, after lunch, Bill rang Theodore to tell him off for not introducing himself to you properly."

"Oh, no." She buried her face in her hands.

"Don't worry about that. Anyway, while Bill was on the phone, Theodore mentioned to him you wrote a letter, and said although your past saddened him, your bravery amazed him."

"He did?"

"The odds were against you from the moment you were placed into foster care, and yet that hasn't stopped you from being successful."

She shook her head. "I'm not successful—not yet."

"Did you say *not yet?* Well, my dear, I don't know how you measure success, but I measure it in a person's determination to achieve their goals and to not give up on their dreams. And if you were hoping to get super rich from your paintings, then I'm afraid to be the bearer of bad news; everybody knows a great artist doesn't hit the jackpot until after they've died." At that, they both laughed.

"I know, I know. Although hitting the jackpot wasn't my goal, it was just to make enough money to do it full time."

"And, what else?"

"There's nothing… else, really."

"Come on. You can tell me."

"Okay, but my answer will disappoint you." June motioned her to carry on. "After accomplishing being a full-time artist, I want to buy a house and get a cat to keep me company. Or maybe, in time, I'll have a dozen, and people will call me a crazy-cat-lady."

"Sounds wonderful and humble, and that perhaps you have achieved your dreams back to front. You have a house and you're more than welcome to get a cat—or a dozen. Although, I'm afraid you'll only be known as a crazy-cat-lady by myself and Bill."

"Well, I don't know. It's not my house and I'm still paying rent on my flat until my one month trial is up, and I don't think Theodore would let me get a cat."

"First, your one-month trial is up. Second, if you're uncertain, ask him if you can have one. Something tells me he wouldn't turn you down."

"My trial is up?" She frowned. "Why wouldn't he turn me down?"

"From our end, it is. However, you're more than welcome to keep us on trial. As for your other question, I will answer it with one of my own: of all the flowers in the world he could have chosen, why red roses?"

* * *

The morning had been busier than the others, and yet it was still the most relaxed she'd ever felt while working. She leaned back in her chair to admire the roses she had moved from the kitchen to her desk, then pulled out a piece of paper from the drawer to write Theodore another letter.

"Or should I ring him?" She put the paper back and drummed the desk. "And make a complete fool of myself?" Surely she would feel more confident speaking to him if they were not face to face? That said, she took the phone off the receiver and put it back a few times before pressing speed-dial.

"No, no," she said, while it rang. What if he was asleep?

He answered. "May I help you with something, Molly?"

Oh, how she loved the way he said her name. "Hi, umm…"

"My name is not Umm."

Did she just hear him laugh? She squeezed the phone to her ear.

"May I help you with something?" he repeated.

"Oh, er, no. I actually phoned you to ask… But first, I would like to apologise if I woke you—"

"You didn't wake me, and it wouldn't be something for you to apologise for if you did. Understood?"

She never imagined he would be this easy-going. "Understood. So… I wanted to thank you for amending the rules and for my roses. They are beautiful. Oh, and the cooker has been installed; I will test it out tonight—before dark." She smiled and hoped he did, too.

"You are very welcome, Molly. Was there something else?" Was that him giving her a cue to hurry? Bill had said he was curt. So, perhaps he wasn't.

"Well, I was speaking to June earlier about getting a cat. She said I could, but I wanted to ask you first." Then, something she dreaded doing, she babbled on. "It's just that I have always wanted one—since I was a child, but being in a flat meant it was near impossible. The tenant on the ground floor had a cat. Well, she had three, actually. But of course, all she had to do was leave her window open for them to come and go as they pleased. I lived in the top-floor flat, you see, so it wouldn't have been fair on the cat." She paused, catching her breath. "But you can say no. It's your house. As you already know and don't need me to tell you that."

This time, there was no mistaking it; she heard him laugh. Her heart melted, for she had not heard a sound more pleasing to her ears. "I'm glad you find me funny."

"In an endearing way. What sort of cat do you want?"

She hadn't expected his question, and took a few seconds to answer. "There isn't a certain breed I lean towards because I wanted to get a rescue cat. I guess, when the time came, I would choose a cat that was most in need. Maybe one that had been in the sanctuary the longest."

"Very well. Consider yourself a cat owner."

"Wow, really? Thank you."

"You deserve it. Although, it would please Bill if your cat wore a bell on its collar."

"Hmm, very cryptic. Did you get that from June or the other way around?"

He laughed and again, making Molly bite her lower lip.

"Bill adores the birds, and the bell on the cat's collar scares them away before they're caught."

"Huh, I always wondered why cats wore bells and dogs didn't. Also, while I'm here, I'm sorry if my letter overstepped. I just wanted you to know you're not alone, that's all."

"Stop apologising, Molly, and feel your confidence grow. As for my parents, it happened many years ago; enough time for me to make peace with their loss. That being said, if you wish to talk about your experience in more depth, I will be here for you."

Her eyes watered. "I'm in the same boat as you and have made peace with my parents' loss, too."

"But not what your grandparents did? Just so you know, it doesn't make you a bad person because you can't forgive them. Perhaps you feel that if you reached out to your grandparents, it would feel as if you are sending them an invitation to enter back into your life. However, you don't have to reach out to them and verbally forgive them for what they did, or rather, didn't do. You can let them go along with the pain you're in by simply saying it to yourself—when you're ready."

"What about the Christmas card they send me every year?" Which was the reason she hated that time of year so much. Not only did that card remind her she was alone, it reminded her why.

"You have a new address, Molly. A fresh start, and soon, a cat."

She smiled at that. "You're right."

"I will let you get on with your day. Phone me whenever you want to."

After she said she would, there was an awkward silence on the line because neither was yet to put the phone down.

Chapter Eight

Theodore couldn't see from his screen what Molly had written on a card she left on the kitchen island, and was eager to read it. As he watched her walk through the hallway and turn towards the stairs, he switched off his monitors and made his way to his.

It pleased him more than it should when he opened his door into the main house and walked through her lavender scent, still lingering in the air. Having her here, this close, had soon become tormenting—as predicted, but her out there would be far worse for him, he decided. He just had to keep a distance between them while making her happy at the same time.

He picked up the note placed next to a plate of biscuits he had watched her bake earlier.

Theodore, these are for you. Lots of love, Molly xx.

Placing the note in his pocket, he then grimaced at the plate before him. If he threw them in the bin, she might find them, and the last thing he wanted to do was hurt her. She'd had her fill of pain. So, he did something he hadn't done in years; he opened the back door and made his way to the cottage to give Bill the biscuits.

* * *

Molly hummed while she got ready for the day. She had spent the evening thinking about what Theodore had said over the phone. Over the years, she had tried to see things from her grandparent's perspective, and had tried in vain to understand why they hadn't taken her in when she needed them the most. Now, she no longer needed to. She had found the strength to forgive her grandparents and let them go—along with the pain that accompanied them. It was now in the past, and she felt a sense of freedom. And as well as feeling uplifted, today was an exciting one. Today she would go online and see what she needed for a cat, make a list, and then head into town to buy everything.

Her phone rang from her bedroom while she was applying her make-up.

"Hi, June. Is everything okay?"

"It is. Theodore rang me first thing this morning, asking me to open the gates for a delivery. I want you to come down now so I can see the look on your face when you see it."

Molly sat on the edge of her bed while she digested what she had said. "A delivery? What is it?"

"Come and see for yourself." She put the phone down.

Molly wore a frown all the way to her door. When she closed it, she saw a note attached to the outside.

Thank you for taking the time to make me biscuits. Lots of love, Theodore xx.

She beamed as she carefully peeled the tape from the door to not rip the note, then went back to her bedroom to add it to the two lists of house rules and the enveloped card in a shoe box.

Her mind was more on the note than the delivery downstairs, and she thought about what she could make him next.

“Molly, hurry,” June called from the main entrance.

So she hopped down the stairs two at a time and jogged through the hallway and saw that June wasn’t alone. Molly looked from the guest to the pet carrier by her feet, then cupped her hands over her face, peeping through her fingers. It couldn’t be? Her chin trembled.

“This is Carol from the local cat sanctuary. She’s here to do a house check before introducing you to your new cat.”

She cleared her throat. “Which is not how we usually conduct adoptions, I have to be honest.”

June’s eyes lit with humour. “No, but I bet it does when you receive a large donation?”

Carol lifted her chin. “Enough to keep us going for countless years and expand.” She looked around the room, then at Molly. “House check approved. Now, I know June said, ‘your new cat’, but you should know she's very old and has been with us for a long time. Which was what Mr Ardelean requested."

"He did?" Molly wiped her eyes. "Can I meet her?"

Carol went down to her knees beside the pet carrier, then Molly did the same. She had never felt such excitement as she opened the door and the cat purred before peeking out.

"Oh, she's beautiful. Perfect." She put her hand close to the black, one-eyed cat so she could sniff her hand.

"You would assume from her appearance she'd come from an abusive background. However, she was much loved until her owner passed away, and has a gentle temperament."

"Is that why she's been with you the longest, because she's missing an eye?" Finally, the cat sniffed her hand, then stepped fully from the carrier to explore her surroundings.

"I would like to think not. Her name is Hallow, short for Halloween, but you can change it."

"No, it suits her." Hallow rubbed her side against her legs and Molly ran her fingers through her soft pelt.

Carol stood. "I will leave you with a week's supply of food and a list of do's and don'ts, but I hope you understand that at her age, your primary job as a first time cat parent is to make her feel comfortable in her final years. Although, hopefully, her new surroundings will give her a new lease of life. You just never know when they're that age."

"She will make a fantastic first time cat parent," June said.

Molly couldn't find the words as she sat crossed legged with Hallow. She couldn't believe one of her dreams had come true, and Theodore was the reason behind it. He did this for her, but why? Was he this generous to everyone in his life, or was she just overthinking it? Was there something between them?

"I'll leave you all to your morning, but first, I'll need a signature for my records." Carol passed the paperwork and pen down to Molly to where she sat, clearly not wanting to disturb them while they bonded.

"I'm already in love with her, and I will make sure she has everything she needs. I promise." She handed the paperwork back up to her.

June led Carol through the door, leaving Molly to follow Hallow as she made her way through to the living room. Then she jumped onto the sofa and curled into a ball.

"I bet you are tired after your morning. I hope you don't mind if I sit next to you and watch you sleep."

June sat opposite her with a huge grin on her face. "She's beautiful, Molly. And I don't need to ask you if you're pleased because your face says it all."

"I can't believe I have a cat," she whispered. "Why would Theodore do this for me? We hardly know each other."

She shrugged. "Maybe if you get to know him, you'll find out the answer to your question."

When she didn't answer—because she wasn't sure how to, June continued, "My dear, the last thing I want to do is ruin your happiness, but I also received a call from the hospital this morning too. It would seem a cancellation has bumped Bill's surgery forward. He's pleased, of course, because he wants it over and done with, but we're leaving this afternoon to get him prepped for tomorrow morning."

"Oh, June. I hope it goes well. I know you're worried—I am too, but he will pull through after his recovery. We'll make sure of it."

She seemed understandably unsure. "I will spend the first and second night with him, then after, I will stay in a hotel only a two-minute drive away until he's discharged."

"And that will be a week?"

June nodded in agreement. "If all goes well. If you need help with anything, leave me a message as I may have my phone off most of the time. I will send you an email with a list of things that need picking up and when, but don't forget you can always contact Theodore with further questions."

"When you can, will you let me know how Bill gets on?"

"Of course." She stood and looked down at Hallow. "She's a lucky cat."

"I'm the lucky one." And that was exactly how she felt.

* * *

Molly said her goodbyes to Bill and June at the end of the drive before their chauffeur closed their door and drove off. She missed them already, but she was also desperate to get back inside so she could continue watching Hallow sleep.

As she was waving until the car was out of sight, her phone rang and she answered it without looking at who the caller was, hoping it was Theodore.

"Hi."

"It's Jackie. You sound chirpy."

No longer would she stutter and mumble. She rang her, so she could do all the talking until Molly decided she had heard enough.

"I'm ringing you to… Where do I start? I'll start with an apology because you were right about James. He came by yesterday, demanding I tell him where you are. Of course, I don't know, and it would be best if I don't. Anyhow, he became aggressive, psychotic, called me every name under the sun and threatened to burn the shop down. I called the police, but I'm not sure what they will do about it. James mentioned you hadn't been home. I suggest you stay away for a while… Hello… Are you still there?"

Molly couldn't believe what she was hearing, or rather she could, she just never expected to hear it from Jackie's mouth. "I'm sorry… No, what I mean is; James is a nasty piece of work. I never called the police because of how manipulative he is." Then she remembered something, something she could have used in her defence. "There are cameras in the shop. Find the footage and take it to the station for evidence."

"You're right. I forgot about those. I am sorry you dealt with that, and I didn't believe you. The way his face changed… It scared me. Did he… you don't have to answer, but did he hit you?"

"No, he only ever pulled my hair, but I knew it could have led to him hitting me. Jackie, make sure he doesn't follow you home by driving back a different way each day, and make some pointless turns until you're satisfied he's not behind you. He doesn't have a driving licence, but I have seen him in three different cars since I broke it off with him."

Molly heard Jackie sniff back tears and even though she knew it wasn't her fault, she couldn't help but feel responsible. "I didn't intend to frighten you, Jackie."

"It's not that. If that fucker follows me while I'm in my car, I'll do an emergency stop, reverse into his bumper and hope he wasn't wearing a seat belt."

Molly smiled despite the situation. She had her hand on the front door handle, but decided not to finish this conversation indoors. The house was fast becoming her haven, and she would not tarnish it with her past.

"Then I hope he is stupid enough to follow you."

Jackie laughed, then sobered. "What I wanted to say was that I'm not just sorry for not believing you, but for the way I treated you. You were a better artist than me, and had achieved what I couldn't. Instead of encouraging you, I blamed you for my shortcomings."

Her words went a long way to healing the rift between them, and Molly applied the same method she had used with her grandparents, by letting the pain of what Jackie had done to her go without sending her an invitation back into her life.

"It's in the past—all forgotten. Jackie, may I ask you to delete my number in case he does somehow get a hold of your phone. He's sneaky and I wouldn't put it past him."

"I will as soon as we hang up, but first, are you okay? Do you have a safe place to stay and money?"

"I am, and I'm living and working in a different town." The lie tasted like acid on her tongue, but it was necessary, just in case Jackie slipped up while in another confrontation with James. "Stay safe. Bye."

After she hung up, she took a few deep breaths to help her push back those negative thoughts and bring forth positivity before she entered the house—her new life. And after another wonderful afternoon, she wrote Theodore a letter, thanking him for everything, slipped it under his door, and made her way upstairs to have another relaxing evening.

It had pleased Molly when Hallow followed her up the stairs and had initially slept in her bed, but now she was scratching at the door to be let out at midnight.

"We're not allowed downstairs. Can't you wait until tomorrow? Your litter-tray is up here. See?" She shook it.

Hallow meowed, and Molly swore it sounded just like she'd said please. She was already under strict instructions to not let Hallow out of the house for the next few weeks. So how could she refuse her when all she wanted to do was to investigate the house? "Okay, but I'll leave the door open."

The cat leapt into the hallway as soon as she opened the door, into the darkness and out of sight. She tilted her head. Why was it so dark? Had she turned the lights off? No, she hadn't because the curtains were always closed. She crept into the hallway, inching closer to the stairs. As she hung over the bannister, her oversized t-shirt rode up, revealing her bare legs. She thought about putting bottoms on before going down, but clearly Theodore had already returned to the basement. So not only would she not get caught, it wouldn't matter that she was wearing next to nothing. And really, hadn't they passed that? Was that rule in particular really necessary? Only one of them was, according to June.

She crept down the stairs, thankful they didn't creak, and made her way to, the best she could, to the main room. A soft light emitted from the office. Meaning he was down here, after all. She stood indecisive before changing her mind—she had too much to lose, and wouldn't risk losing her job and cat.

She turned, bumped into a wall, then screamed when—what she thought was the wall—said, "Lights."

They all came on simultaneously, blinding her. When her eyes adjusted, she saw Theodore casually leaning on the door frame with Hallow curled around his ankle. "Is it a full moon tonight?"

"I… I don't know."

He bent down to stroke Hallow behind her ears, then as he stood, his gaze locked on to her feet, and travelled up her legs until he found her eyes. "It's not. Which means you're breaking the rules."

Her attempt to not apologise ended up with her going on the defensive. "All the rules are stupid, anyway. Apart from one."

He smiled. "I wonder who said that. Very well, all the rules are stupid apart from one. However, you will abide by them."

"What about Hallow? I didn't know where she was."

"Cats like to explore at night because they are nocturnal. If you were to leave your door ajar, she would have returned to you before you woke." He stepped closer to her. "Good night, Molly."

The way he looked at her legs and his demeanour now made her feel in control of the situation and gave her the strength to take a step closer. "What would happen if I didn't go upstairs? Would I really lose my job?"

He closed the distance between them, making her tremble with nervousness and anticipation. She crossed one knee over the other, trying to dampen the desire she felt for him, in case she was reading the situation wrong. When he curled a finger under her chin and tilted her head up, she uncrossed her legs and splayed her hands on his chest.

"I could show you what would happen. I'm warning you; there will be no going back for either of us if I do."

Her hand ran up his chest to his neck. "Show me."

Chapter Nine

Theodore couldn't have asked for more when he picked her up and she wrapped her legs around his waist. They looked at each other, as if it were for the first time, and when he sensed her passion overriding her nervousness, he lowered them onto the floor and hooked his hand behind Molly's knee, keeping her open to him. He hadn't kissed a human before, so he brushed her lips with his, then travelled to her neck before she had time to discover his fangs with her tongue.

Even though he felt her rapid pulse in his mouth, she melted beneath him. Then she became demanding, holding his head in place. When she tightened her legs around him, he let go of her knee, ran his hand up her leg, and pushed her t-shirt up past her breasts. Her skin was softer than silk and her breasts felt as beautiful as he imagined they would, so he pulled his mouth away from her neck, needing to see them, needing to put his mouth on more of her.

"You are everything, Molly."

"Kiss me." Her fingers scraped his scalp, urging him closer.

Yes. No. What should he do? Blind her with pleasure. As his lips inched closer to hers, his hand brushed over her stomach, then lower. She arched her back when he massaged a finger inside and thrust his tongue into her mouth. He growled in approval when he felt her walls already clenching around his finger. She was highly responsive to his touch, and he would use that to his advantage. Then her hands fumbled with the buttons of his shirt, wanting it off, but he couldn't oblige her yet. She was close to coming, and he didn't want to stop.

She quivered beneath him, and when eyes fluttered closed and her head flew back, he knew he had her where he wanted and slipped another finger inside in time to feel ripples of bliss pulse through her body. "That's it. Feel me inside you and know now that there will be no one other than me."

"Yes," she breathed.

To hide his teeth, he kept his mouth close to her neck when he smiled wide, and wondered if he could get her to agree to everything when she was this aroused. He put his theory to the test by running his tongue over her nipple. "You want me?"

"Yes."

He straightened to take his shirt off, and delighted in the fact she was eager to see what he would reveal. When she bit her lip and her gaze darted all over his chest, then down to the top button of his trousers, her approval of him filled him with pride. He then ran his hand down the inside of her leg, then stopped, teasing her. “You want me inside you?”

“Yes.”

After he unbuttoned his trousers, he entered her again with his fingers, then stopped. “You want my cock inside you, making you want me more.”

She shuffled closer to him with hooded eyes. “Yes.”

Watching her watch him with lust in her eyes pleased him more than he had ever been, furthering his own arousal before crawling back up her body, between her legs. When his tip brushed her centre, they both inhaled. He knew from having his fingers in her his cock was too big and may cause discomfort, so he’d go slow, gently rock himself inside her until she urged him for more.

“Wait,” she said. “I’m not on anything. Do you have a condom?”

Telling her vampires couldn’t breed with humans until after they had transitioned was not an option, but he didn’t feel disappointed. He would have her tonight in other ways—and made a bet with himself she would soon give in to him. So for now, he would have to humour her. He shook his head. “No.”

She let out a steady breath and seemed disheartened, but he’d soon wipe that look off her face.

“The floor is no place for our first time, anyway.” He stroked her hair back from her face, then brought a lock to his nose. Under her enchantment, his next words came out before he thought them through. “My bed or yours?”

"We can't." She ran her fingers along his jaw. "Wait. Did you say your bed? In the basement?"

He turned away before laughing, but he now needed to find the words to discourage her from choosing his bed. "We won't do anything you don't want to, but understand this: whichever bed you choose, you won't be sleeping, either. You also have the added danger of me locking you in my basement if you choose my bed, so perhaps yours sounds more appealing to you, agreed?"

She looked excited by this, and it made his heart swell for her even though he'd clearly lost this round. He also noted another advantage over her other than her passion: her curiosity.

"I choose your bed."

"Are you certain? With no sleep and potential imprisonment." He picked her up off her feet, forcing her to wrap her legs around him for balance. He turned in a circle. "Take one last look around. It might be your last."

She giggled. "Who will pick up your clothes tomorrow if I'm locked away?"

"We don't need clothes where we're going."

"Oh, no. I walked straight into that one, didn't I?" She put a hand over her face, then when he stood outside his door, she turned and looked at the keypad lock.

"It's the same code as the front door. Go on."

She wore a grin, but her trepidation showed when her hand shook over the keypad. As soon as it opened, she craned her neck to see further, so he let her slide down his body and explore by herself.

When they stepped off the last step of the stairs, he squeezed her bum. "Do you often walk around my house naked?"

She faced him, ran her finger from his chest, over his abdomen, down to his hilt. "Do you?"

He pulled her to him and kissed her. "It wouldn't take me long to change the code for the lock so you couldn't leave."

Little did she know he wasn't joking, so she laughed and made her way down his hallway. "I can't see anything."

But he could, as clear as day. "Lights," he said. There weren't as many down here as upstairs—he didn't need them. At least they wouldn't be a shock to her eyes like they had been earlier.

"I don't know where to look first. It's huge down here." She said, walking into the centre of his open plan living quarters. He stayed where he was, wanting to see her naked and among his things. Then she pulled a blanket off his sofa and wrapped it around herself.

She looked at him sheepishly. "I'm cold. So, this is your living room, your bedroom is over there, gym over there, bathroom is through that door because I can see a towel on the floor, and I take it, from the blue light coming from over the top of that door, that your office is in there. So, where's your kitchen?"

Molly had clocked another staircase before walking into his main living area—stairs that led down to a lower level. She wanted to ask him about it, but he was yet to answer her first question and tell her where his kitchen was.

She tightened the blanket around her as more chills pricked her skin. The way he looked at her from across the room as if she were prey filled her with fear and excitement. She wanted him and he seemed to want her like no man had ever before, giving her the confidence she had felt to walk around naked. And if it wasn't for him not having a condom, she would have let him take her on the floor. While his muscled body surrounded her, she could not think of anything else other than having him inside her. So what's changed? Everything.

As she looked around his private quarters, the remaining pieces of the puzzle slotted into place against her wishes. Now that she was on the receiving end of his kindness, tasted his kisses, came over his fingers, she wasn't sure she wanted to know the truth. The fact she still wanted him regardless, frightened her more than who or what Theodore really was. Also, why didn't he frighten her if what she suspected was true? Perhaps it was because the truth was impossible, she decided, and then searched for an alternative to what had been right in front of her this whole time.

She walked over to his DVD collection and ran her finger over the spines, then she ran her fingertips over the graze she felt on her neck. Without looking at him, she made her way to his library and saw his books were in the same theme and genre as the DVDs. Pulling the blanket away from her chest, she saw two parallel dents in her skin above her nipple. Maybe he was just a fanatic? Do fanatics go to the same lengths and extremes as he does to live out this sort of fantasy? He was still him: kind, generous and sexy as hell. And wasn't it common knowledge that the wealthy were sometimes eccentric? That theory didn't quite fit with his personality, though, did it? Although, her other theory didn't quite fit with reality. Yet, only one theory was the truth.

With a heavy heart, Molly turned to him. "Where's your kitchen?"

Theodore knew she was on the cusp of discovering his secret and stood before her to unwrap the blanket, then re-wrapped it around them both, keeping her close to him. Preventing her from running away from him if she tried to. "It's upstairs."

"Why didn't you have a cooker when I moved in? How did you cook your food?"

"I don't cook." He could tell she didn't accept that and although it looked as if she had let it go, he was old enough to know she hadn't and would try from a different angle.

She turned and leaned her back into his chest. "Did you like those biscuits I made for you?"

He tightened his grip before kissing the top of her head. "I appreciated the time you took to make them for me."

"Hmm. Did you taste the cinnamon I put in them?"

When he nibbled the top of her ear, he hoped she would still respond to him. And she did. Her head fell to the side, as he made his way to her neck. “I prefer the taste of you above all others.”

“Why was there food in the fridge when I arrived?”

“It got delivered the day before you moved in because you need food to sustain you.”

“And you don’t?”

When he ignored her, she put her hand behind her back, found his cock, then stroked him. “You want to be inside me?”

“Yes,” he said, finding her centre, running his fingers between her folds. “Yes.”

She steadied her hand. “How is it you became the owner of the biggest blood donation organisation in the world?”

“Don’t stop.”

She continued to stroke, then stopped again. “Answer me.”

Molly was using the same tactics he had used against her and she seemed determined to beat him at his own game. He could not have been prouder of her, and it pleased him also because it meant she wasn’t frightened of him. But humans can be unpredictable, which meant her demeanour could change at any second when the truth sunk in, and he knew now he would have to have her before she wore him down and he confessed. He dropped the blanket, ran his other hand down her back, then used his fingers to enter her from behind while his fingers from the front moved up to massage her breasts. She shifted her hips, wanting to feel more of him, then began stroking him.

"Answer me." Her breathing became heavy.

"I will," he said, smiling wide before guiding her to her knees. "Don't stop touching me."

"Who are you? Really?" She quickened her hand.

He responded by quickening his, too. She groaned and then fell to her hands, making him growl in triumph before he positioned himself over her to whisper in her ear. "Do you want me inside you?"

She moaned then shook her head. "Tell me who you are? Or what you are?"

He nudged her knees further apart with his and positioned himself to take her. "You're about to come. So close. Tell me you want me inside you."

"No."

He took his hand away, ending her build up, and she turned to her back whilst beneath him and looked up at him accusingly. "You wouldn't."

"You will tell me what I want to hear." He picked her up and took her to his bed, taking only a second to burn the image of her lying there into his mind before he positioned himself between her legs. He re-entered her with his fingers, massaging her until her head fell back. Then he stopped again. "Tell me what I want to hear."

"Theodore, please." She tried to move his hands out of the way so she could touch herself, needing release.

Knowing and not caring his fangs were now on display, he smiled before grabbing both of her wrists, then he held them above her head. "You know what I am." He teased her entrance with the tip of his cock.

"Say it," she breathed, widening her legs and arching her back.

When he pulled back, she tried to shuffle towards him, making him smile freely. "Tell me what I want to hear, then I will say it."

She growled in frustration. "I want you."

"You want me where?"

"Inside me."

He kissed her and felt her moan in his mouth as he entered her slowly, stretching her, as he knew he would, until he filled her completely. "My beautiful Molly," he breathed.

Her eyes squeezed shut as she became accustomed to his size. After the tension left her body, he pushed himself in even further before coming out, then picked up speed. As he rocked faster, taking her to the edge, she locked him in place with her legs. While she was on the brink of another orgasm, he said, "What am I?"

"What?" She was breathless.

"What am I?"

"I don't care what you are."

When he slowed down, the look of betrayal in her expression made him smile. "Answer me," he said, then slowing down again.

"A vampire. You're a vampire."

Then he picked up the pace until her nails bit into his back and she screamed out his name.

Chapter Ten

Passion, his scent, his body, his laugh and even his bloody accent had blinded Molly. Yet as she lay, fully sated, she didn't feel like a loser in the game they'd just played. Torn between needing to sleep and interrogating her new prize, she rubbed her eyes open and let out a steady breath. "Tell me everything."

Theodore propped himself against his headboard, pulled her over his chest and stoked her hair, folding a lock of it behind her ear. "You asked me how I became the owner of the largest blood donation organisation in the world. The answer is that my father created it many years ago."

Molly was still on the fence regarding her two theories—even after seeing his fangs. After all, people can get them done at the dentist these days. Yet, she knew the truth in her heart. He looked otherworldly with his flawless skin and bright eyes. He moved unlike that of a human—like a ghost, gliding rather than rigid motions. And he was unusually strong. The memory of him lifting and carrying her as if the rules of gravity didn't apply to them would never leave her.

"How many years ago did your father create it?"

"Before I go any further, you need to understand that I would sooner die a thousand deaths than hurt you."

"How many years ago?" She looked up to face him.

A sigh of relief escaped from him, but she wasn't sure why. "A few thousand years ago, humans referred to us as gods. Human sacrifices began in our honour, and although it wasn't what we all wanted, the humans were willing. After many people needlessly died, my father worked alongside the humans to find a more sustainable way for us to coexist. It started with switching innocent people with criminals for sacrifices, then as the world changed and the technology became available, blood donation."

"What did you mean when you said they needlessly died?"

"When we feed, we don't need to do it until the point of death, but the humans back then, thought that by dying—sacrificing themselves—we would bring them good fortune, and thought it would end droughts, that their crops would flourish and that it would cure diseases. Some vampires even let them believe it for their convenience."

Molly needed a second for her mind to adjust to understand the information she just received. What she thought was that there were good and bad vampires—as there were with humans. Then she thought that perhaps her mind was just trying to protect itself by searching for similarities between humans and vampires.

He crushed her to him. "Say something. Actually, I have something to say. How did you put it all together as quickly as you did?"

"Curtains, something Bill said, cooker, organisation, sending blood bags to personal addresses, something else Bill said, June's minor slip ups—whether or not intentional, and you." She poked her finger past his lips and lifted the top one up. "There's only one thing telling me that this isn't true and that you're more of a fanatic than the real thing, and that's your DVD and book collection."

"My DVD collection?" he said, while she scraped his teeth with her nail.

"They are all vampire films. I know, because I've seen some of them. Why do you have so many? Are you so obsessed with them you want to be one?"

"No, I'm not obsessed with my kind. I have them because many of my associates wrote and directed those films."

"Even the black and white ones?"

He nodded. "Yes, and I know who created the very first vampire film."

"Why would they do that?" Then she answered her own question. "To make us more susceptible. Are you planning on revealing yourselves? How come humans knew about your kind's existence and now we don't? How old are you?"

He laughed. “I don’t know which of your questions to answer first. Two of them will need a detailed explanation. So I’ll answer the last one first. I’m seven-hundred years old.” The grip he had on her tightened. “Molly, you must keep this information to yourself. This house isn’t just my home, it is a sacred place which contains tablets, scrolls and books about our history. I wouldn’t want to burn it to the ground to protect our secret.”

“No one would believe me, anyway. Have you ever killed anyone? Even though you said no one needed to die.”

“I can if I want. There’s an organisation that runs alongside mine called Iustitia, named after the Roman goddess of justice. My kind track and trace known criminals and flag them, so that the ones who prefer to hunt can target those humans. Drinking blood outside of mine or the high council’s organisation is against our laws.”

“And what if I were to have a nosebleed or graze my knee? Wouldn’t that make you want to… break that law?”

“It would be no different to you walking past a coffee shop and smelling the aromas. It might make you want a coffee, but you wouldn’t dive in and start tearing the coffee bean bags open with your teeth.”

She laughed with him, then went back to her questions. “Are the laws ever broken? If so, what happens when they are?”

“Yes, and as a council member, I oversee the case and determine the punishment. If the vampire in question can prove the human was a criminal and didn't contribute to society, then they would receive a warning. If an innocent dies, we imprison the vampire for fifty years and we donate their wealth to either the family members of the deceased or to a charity."

"Are all vampires wealthy?"

"When you are immortal, it rains money. It wasn't hard for us to secure castles and land thousands of years ago, only for it to be handed down to the next generation. Or for my kind to join a royal family by marriage, then become the last member standing because they didn't produce any heirs."

Molly filed that last statement away. "And like the humans who wanted to sacrifice themselves for you, everything was freely given?"

"Of all the animals mother nature has created, the predators are the most alluring, making it easier for them to catch their prey. Humans are inherently attracted to us and want to please us."

"How many of your kind are there?"

"Three million. Even though we are immortal, we don't breed like humans—rabbits."

"You don't breed like humans because you can't breed with them?" She didn't wait around for his answer, instead, she nodded her head and then tried to get out of bed. She needed to think, and then think some more—maybe over a coffee. No, she needed something stronger.

"Don't." He took her hand and pulled her back to him. "It's easier this way, now that you know."

She pulled back and stood by the edge of the bed, her legs trembled, but not from terror. Thoughts of him pulling her hair the way James had done were fleeting for she knew he would not treat her that way, but that didn't mean he was completely free of wrongdoing "When were you going to tell me?"

"I wasn't planning on telling you. I created the house rules so you wouldn't find out."

His eyes had pleaded for mercy before he answered and she tutted, knowing now she could never stay angry with him. She ran her hands over her face. "I felt your teeth when we kissed and saw them when you smiled." She pointed to the ceiling. "Which I first noticed upstairs, not down here after you got what you wanted. And now, after inspecting them, I know they're real. What were you going to say when I asked you about them?"

"I wouldn't have answered you," he answered honestly.

"So when people ask about your teeth, you just blank them?"

"I'm out of touch. The only humans I see are my daughter- and son-in-law—"

"Your what?" This time when she stepped back, he leapt off the bed.

"June is my daughter. I adopted her. Come back to me, Molly." He pulled her into him and locked her in place with one arm around her shoulders and the other around her waist..

"For fuck's sake, Theodore."

“Don’t swear.” His tone was commanding. A tone he had no right to use with her after what she’d just learned.

“I just found out that you're a mythical monster everyone either wants or wants to be. So I will fucking swear if I want to.”

“Enough,” he barked.

“Fucker.” She twisted her body out from his grip and ran across the room.

“Come here.” He went after her and pulled her back to his chest then slapped her bum.

“Ow.” She turned and faced him, and it pained her to see his expression was one of regret and fear, vanquishing her anger and replacing it with forgiveness. Then her anger returned, and she marched to the side of him and slapped his bum.

He looked bewildered and her instant reaction was a burst of laughter, then she started giggling. Had she really just slapped a vampire? A vampire she’d just slept with? A vampire she wanted to sleep with again, and again—even though she was still sore from his size. Her giggling fit started all over again.

“This is far from funny, Molly. Have you lost your mind?”

“Yes, I have lost my mind. We’re standing in your living room, naked, and slapping each other on the bum. Oh, but before that, I found out what you are. Tell me which part of this isn’t funny.” Feeling exposed and needing comfort, she pulled her hair around from her back to cover her breasts.

"Here." He smiled before bending down to grab the blanket from the floor, then handed it to her. "Take this."

"Thank you. You have a devastating smile, by the way. Teeth included." She wrapped the blanket over her shoulders. "Where do we go from here? I feel I need time to digest this, to... understand what this means."

He stepped in her space, and he put his arms around her waist. "We want each other, yes? Admit that and then the rest will fall into place."

She buried her face in his chest, breathing him in, then looked up at him. Yes, she wanted him. How could she not? She brushed his fringe from his eyes. "I do want you. But I have so many questions."

Theodore shut his eyes in a silent prayer before he kissed her. "Spend the night with me. Let me worship you before you ask me your questions."

"Hmm, tempting, but no. Do you think I didn't notice the other railing leading to another level below this one before we turned into this room? You could have other women down there—locked away. And what if you got me pregnant? Would I give birth to a flock of bats?"

He threw his head back laughing. "You are not what I expected, Molly. As for you being pregnant, it's impossible, I'm afraid. Like you said; we don't breed like humans because we can't breed with them."

"I thought so."

"How about we will meet in the middle. Spend the night with me, asking me questions—as many as you want, until you feel more comfortable around me."

Her eyes widened, because although she couldn't wrap her mind over what he was, she was comfortable around him. She felt safe with him. Proving her theory, she stepped back, and just as she thought he wouldn't let her go, he did and she took another step back, Then she casually walked around his living quarters, making a note of his belongings, and lack of. She ran her hand over the stone walls. Where was his art? It wasn't unusual for your bedroom to be decorated differently to the rest of the house, but surely there should be some similarities. She glanced back at Theodore and it looked like he was trying to read her mind. Good luck with that, she projected.

"I want to see what's below the basement?" She pointed at the floor.

He closed the distance between them. "I'll show you—if you agree to spend the rest of the night with me."

* * *

Molly had agreed to his terms, not because he blackmailed her, but because she wanted to. Everything he did, his movements, his hair, his body, his choice of words, enthralled her. And most of all, his need to make her happy and feel comfortable was soon becoming addictive. She'd never experienced that before. Even when he crossed a line by trying to dress her in his clothes, she still burned it to her memory.

"I can do it," she said, zipping up the hoodie he gave her. "You know, it wouldn't have taken me a minute to grab my own clothes."

"I didn't want to give you a chance to back out of our bargain."

She laughed nervously. "When you say things like that, I'm not sure if you're joking."

"Then allow me to clear up that uncertainty of yours: I wasn't joking."

He smiled in a way that dared her to say what she thought about that, then walked across his room to the top of the staircase. Then he motioned her as if he was saying, 'ladies first'.

Molly looked down the stairs and saw another keypad lock on the door below. She nibbled her lip and reached for her hair. "Can I trust you, Theodore?"

"I don't think it matters whether you can trust me. Your curiosity will override caution, convincing you that you can. It is your strength and downfall. A double-edged sword you are yet to master."

"What do you mean?" She wasn't sure if she should be offended by that.

"It's an admirable trait to want to discover the truth, to see things for what they really are and not live a life with blinkers on, but it can be dangerous, too. What if I said that there really is a danger of you being locked in a cage, where you will be forced to give birth to my flock of bats along with the many other women I have down there? I believe you would still want to see for yourself, wouldn't you?"

"Did you give the women roses and cats before you locked them up, too?"

He grinned before kissing her. "Go down and ask them."

She stepped back before bending over to laugh with her hands over her face. "Stop it. I'm not sure if I want to see it now."

"You don't want to meet my winged children?"

"Now that, I would like to see. Something tells me they'd be super cute. Has June been down there?" Asking about June brought her back to reality. No, not reality, just back to the craziness of the situation she had found herself in.

Theodore must have sensed her turmoil because seriousness replaced his playfulness before he answered. "June, as you will understand, was homeschooled, and her history lessons took place down there."

"History lessons? You mean, vampire history?"

"If it helps, our history is intertwined with human history. Some of the most prominent figures in our past and present are vampires. Royalty, high society, politicians,"—he looked pointedly at her—"artists."

"No. Really? Well, I suppose you did say your associates wrote and directed those films. How did they do it without being discovered?"

He ran his fingers through her hair. "We don't have to go down if you don't want to."

"Oh, I wasn't stalling. I just have so many questions." She took two steps down, then looked behind her. "Are you coming?"

He looked pleased with her before he followed. “It’s the same code as the front door.”

She opened the door and stood at the threshold, unable to move her legs. Then she felt Theodore's hands run from her hips to her stomach, then back to her hips. “You don’t have to discover everything all at once. There’s always tomorrow, the next day or whenever you’re ready.”

She breathed out a steady breath, then walked forward into the darkness. The smell was fresh, as well as the air, reminding her of a frosty morning.

When Theodore said lights, she closed her eyes. He was probably right—she didn’t have to discover everything all at once, but she knew herself well enough to know she wouldn’t be able to sleep or do anything else if she didn’t. She opened her eyes. “Hmm, I wasn’t expecting this.”

“Are you disappointed that it’s not a love dungeon? You’re not that type of woman are you?”

She smirked. “I should hope it’s not a love dungeon if you taught your daughter in here.”

“Touché, Molly, looks like I walked into that one.”

She loved how he copied her phrases, but yet again, the mention of June made her head spin. The new world she had entered only hours ago was easy to get lost in, and June was her lifeline back to the old world, so to speak. And yet she wasn’t because she was connected to Theodore. Her head pounded when she couldn’t wrap her mind around him having a daughter older than him—except she wasn’t, was she?

"Umm, I would never call you a liar, but I have to be honest. I can't see… I can't comprehend… It's hard to explain why, but it's as if June is a barrier, preventing me from fully believing this. But then, I remember the things she and Bill have said, and then I can, I suppose. Because they're not a part of my reality, they're a part of yours, aren't they?" She groaned while rubbing her temples. "Oh, I don't know."

"It is a lot of information to take in. The world, as you know, has been turned upside down. That being said, you have done exceptionally well so far. It took Bill nearly twenty years to come to terms with what I am." He grinned.

"Really? I wish they weren't away for the week. It would have gone a long way in helping me understand this. And again, I'm not saying I don't believe you. Well, you know what I mean, don't you?"

"I do know, and it's okay. You need to go at your own pace."

She nodded, then walked into another open spaced room, even bigger than upstairs, and turned in circles, taking it all in. "So, to me, this looks like a museum."

"Technically, it is a museum. A time capsule."

Glass cabinets lined the walls and contained scrolls, clay tablets, knives and jewellery. Even the books were behind glass. Everything except for a large twelve seater table.

"What's this used for? Obviously, I know what a table and chairs are used for, but why do you have one this size? Do you have dinner guests? No, I mean… Umm—" She sidestepped and reached for her hair.

"It's okay. You're half right. Look at me." He curled a finger under her jaw, keeping her in place. "I never want you to feel unsure of yourself around me. Do you understand?"

She kissed him, unable to help herself. "I do."

"Is it a bad time to tell you off for not using proper words?"

"Yes, it is." She tutted, then looked up adoringly at him for making her feel at ease once again. "How was I half right?"

"I host council meetings here once a month. You see that other door over there?" he pointed to the far corner of the room. "That door leads to the outside of the house, on the other side of the turret. The code to that lock is the same as the gate."

"I'm torn between asking what the meetings are about and asking why I'm not allowed in the turret—the library. Or am I allowed in there now, now that I know what you are?"

Theodore pulled a chair out for her, then took a seat. "I will tell you anything you want to know and show you anything you want to see. I promise. That being said, the library is still off limits. I'm not ready to talk about it, and I don't know if I ever will be."

It was obvious to her, since it was his mother's favourite room in the house, that he had not made peace with the loss of his parents like he had said. His openness made her heart pound for him, but he needed her compassion, not her desire. She reached across the table and took his hand in her. “Tell me about the secret meetings, then.”

Chapter Eleven

Molly yawned into her fist again and then used that hand to prop her head up after Theodore told her about the council meetings held at the table they were sitting on. And even though countless hours had passed, she couldn't believe she could fall asleep after discovering myths and legends were now a part of her reality and with so many questions yet to ask.

"So, the sun doesn't kill you, or hurt you in any way other than blinding you?"

"Correct. Our eyes are designed to see in the dark as clearly as you can see in the day. Anything lighter than what's on in this room causes blindness."

"Then why would your associates create films and books that imply the sun is your weakness?"

He smiled at this. "If we are discovered, it helps humans to become more accepting of us if they believe we have many weaknesses. Think back to all the questions you have asked me. You've asked them because of what you think you know about us from watching those films."

"That's true. But I wouldn't have discovered what you are if not for them, either. If secrecy is imperative to your survival, you should mention in your next council meeting that those films are—in your words—a double-edged sword."

Pride shone in his eyes. "I have always said that, and yet there didn't seem to be an alternative. However, you're not frightened of me, and are asking me questions instead of running out the door, so I would have to agree with my associates on this occasion."

"Perhaps if you were someone else, I would have been frightened. So, what are your weaknesses?"

He pulled her chair closer to his. "Why do you want to know? Are you planning on plunging a stake into my heart while I sleep?"

She leaned over the arm of her chair and kissed him. "No, of course not. I just want to know everything."

Theodore had already explained that he didn't eat food—something she already guessed, but he could drink black coffee and alcohol if he really wanted to, but only for the taste. He said his metabolism was too fast to feel the effects of alcohol and caffeine. Only blood sustained him, and yet he couldn't starve. When she asked him what would happen if he went without blood for a long period, he explained that his body would go into hibernation, and that only a single drop of blood was needed to revive him. Then he explained how some vampires hibernated and relied on others to wake them in a specific year.

"Good, because my life has just got interesting, and a stake in the heart would only piss me off."

Molly straightened in her chair. "You just swore. If you can swear and I can't, that makes you a chauvinist."

He laughed. "I'm a chauvinistic vampire. What are you going to do about it?"

"Eat raw garlic before kissing you."

Theodore stood and Molly couldn't guess what he was planning to do until he peeled her from her chair, cradled her in his arms, then sat back down. "Garlic isn't a weakness either."

She snuggled into him and yawned again. "I'll get straight to the point: what kills you?"

"Decapitation or we can die from a broken heart."

She looked up at him. "A broken heart?"

"Yes." He kissed her temple. "You need to sleep."

"I won't be able to—not yet. May I ask how your parents died?" As soon as the question left her lips, she remembered what he had said about the library, and she regretted it. "Don't answer. I shouldn't have asked."

"It's okay. Someone decapitated my father and then my mother died of a broken heart."

If his father died that way, it meant someone killed him. And although she wanted to know why, she would save that question and ask June instead.

"Are you not going to ask me about it?" he said.

"I don't want you to relive what happened by telling me why he died."

"Perhaps it's for the best. The reason *that thing* murdered him would only open up a whole new world to you, and I think you need to take one step at a time into it."

Hearing him say '*that thing*' and '*murdered*' awakened her more than any amount of coffee ever could. How could he say it as casually as he did? Yet, he did tell her it happened many years ago. Still, how does someone move on from that? As for him saying a whole new world would be opened up to her by explaining how his father died; surely that ship had sailed? However, she wouldn't pry.

Wanting to lighten up the conversation, she asked, "When and why did you adopt June?"

The question made him smile, and she couldn't wait to hear him speak about his fond memories.

"There was a time when I often left my home to oversee and help with health screening before extracting blood. Anyway, in some countries, people are paid for their blood—which often attracts drug addicts wanting money for their habit. While I was examining a woman who was clearly an addict, she left her newborn baby in the waiting area amongst other addicts. She couldn't care less about her child's safety, and when I asked about her baby, she asked me how much I would give her for her baby's blood."

Molly gasped and couldn't believe how casually he'd said it. "Poor June. I never would have guessed that's how her life started. So how did she come into your care and not be put up for adoption or put into foster care?"

"I alerted the authorities and told the mother what I had done. She didn't seem to care and said she needed money. So, I gave her the change in my pocket and then off she went. After ten hours, I realised the authorities weren't coming, and that the baby was going to be another child destined to slip through the nets. So when June—although that wasn't her name back then—started crying, I comforted her. While she was in my arms, she kept smiling up at me despite being covered in cuts, bruises and filth, and her strength amazed me. I admire strength and a strong bond formed between us."

Molly wiped her tears away with the sleeve of her borrowed hoodie. "Can you imagine what would have happened to her if you weren't there?"

"Unfortunately, I have lived long enough to see what happens time and time again. Thinking about what could have happened to my daughter is unbearable."

Again, wanting to lighten the mood, she asked, "What was her name before you named her June?"

"I don't know. The mother never said."

"Well, you chose a lovely name for her. What made you choose it?"

His lips curved. "She came into my care in June. It was either that, Monday or Vegas."

She mirrored his smile. "She was born in Vegas? How did you get there and back?"

"The same way you would get there and back: by plane."

Trying to think outside of the box was the only way Molly could wrap her mind around what she had discovered, but clearly, she'd gone too far beyond the box this time. “I couldn’t imagine you flashing your passport at an airport, but then I realised you’d fly private as soon as the words left my lips. Am I right?”

“That’s right. I own a private airfield five miles from town.”

“I know the one you're talking about, but I thought it was a military base.” She shifted in his lap so she could rest her head on his shoulder.

“It’s a medical base. Air ambulances are maintained and fuelled there for deliveries of medical supplies or emergencies. *Where the public is concerned*, it is owned by the military.”

“If you can fly anywhere around the world, why don’t you leave the house anymore to explore?”

“I’ve seen the world ten times over. Where have you explored, or would like to explore?”

Her eyes felt heavy. “I have never left the country, and don’t know where I’d like to go. I guess I’ve never thought about it, knowing,”—she yawned—“it would never happen because I could never afford it. So, that’s why you don’t leave the house; because you’ve seen it all before? Bill seems to think it’s more than that.”

“I also stopped leaving the house because when I did, I was reminded about how fast the world moved on and that I had no one to share it with while it did. Name a place—anywhere, and I will take you there.”

His voice merged with the in-between stages of being awake and asleep, and she wasn't sure if she'd heard him correctly or whether he had said it at all.

Theodore looked down at Molly nestled in his lap, fast asleep. She hadn't asked him what the time was, and he was grateful for it because it was three o'clock in the afternoon, and if she discovered she had forgotten to feed Hallow, she would feel guilty about it. Something he never wanted her to feel. He lifted her back up to his living quarters and placed her in his bed, and sat beside her for a few minutes, not wanting to leave. It was as if this was a dream and that if he left her, it would be akin to waking up from it. And yet, he had to—for her.

"I will be right back," he whispered, knowing she couldn't hear him.

When he got to the stairs that led to the main house, he looked back at her before he made his way up them and was pleased to see Hallow outside the basement door.

"Good afternoon, Cat. Follow me if you want breakfast."

After he fed her, he phoned June to ask about how Bill's surgery went. She said it had gone well, but he could still hear her heart breaking over the phone. He felt useless because he couldn't do anything to ease her pain. Nor could he ease his own where they were both concerned. They were in their mid sixties, and though they could quite easily have another happy and healthy thirty years ahead of them, their life cycle had peaked many years ago and was now in decline. He shook his head to clear it, then rolled up some paperwork and used it to wedge the basement door open so Hallow could come and go as she pleased.

Finally, he was back by Molly's side. Her eyes were moving under her eyelids—a sign she was dreaming, and he thought about undressing her to make her more comfortable, then decided against it. She may have seemed as if she had handled the truth of what he was extremely well, but after she'd slept on it, the shock of what she discovered might catch up with her, and the last thing he wanted was for her to wake up naked and feel exposed. So instead, he retrieved the blanket he had wrapped around them from the night before and draped it over her.

The once generic blanket now held meaning to him—as did his life. Wondering what else would comfort her when she woke, he went to retrieve Hallow, only to find she was already on her way down the stairs. He picked her up and placed her next to Molly and was pleased when she rolled into a ball beside her head and closed her eyes to join her in slumber. Then he went upstairs to retrieve a kettle, a mug, coffee and milk, and placed it on his bedside table.

What else would she want? Her clothes, her art supplies, her phone and everything else she moved in with? No. he wouldn't be doing it to make her feel more comfortable, he would be doing it so she wouldn't have a reason to leave his basement. Still, he should do it. Or not. He mustn't forget that she was yet to fully understand the vampire way.

Humans and their emotions were now more complex than they had ever been in the past. Moulded by social media and what society deemed right or wrong, making things more complicated than they had to be. Especially where relationships were concerned. Where love was concerned. In what world did one live in, where you are taught not to tell someone you loved them because it was too soon? Or a world in which you didn't fully commit because it had become a trend to 'date' multiple people at the same time?

Vampires were simple creatures that took what they wanted and said what they meant. He decided he would do his best to understand and accommodate her complexities the best he could. After all, he knew she would try her best to understand him—it was in her nature to do so. It was another one of her strengths, and why he had done what he had done.

Theodore had taken Molly as his bride. He had wed her with their first kiss and had consummated the marriage on this very bed. She was his and he hers, regardless of whether she transitioned. They would spend the rest of her human years together here, or wherever in the world she wanted to go, and when the time came for her to part from this world, he would die like his mother—from a broken heart.

Now that he was certain of the future, he lay beside her, pulled her back to his chest, and told her something he had always known since the first time he saw her painting his home. "I love you."

* * *

When Molly woke, it felt like she was still dreaming while still snuggled in Theodore's hoodie and with his arm around her, holding her close to him.

Then she bolted upright. "Oh, no. I haven't fed Hallow."

Theodore ran his hand down her back. "I have done it. She's had breakfast, and she was here until I gave her dinner. Now, she is exploring."

She rubbed her eyes open. "I need to phone June and ask how Bill's surgery went."

He reached past her and flipped the kettle on. Was she still dreaming? Why was there a kettle on his side table? Then, like a tidal wave, last night's events hit her. She broke the rules, they kissed, she discovered what he was; he didn't deny it; they had mind blowing sex and then they went into a large room below the basement where she asked him a thousand questions and had twice as many more to ask.

"His surgery went well. The doctors woke him up to check his vitals and now he is resting. At this time, June will be asleep too. Relax, Molly." He ran his thumb over her brow to smooth out her worry lines.

She let out a sigh of relief and rubbed her eyes again. "Thank you for feeding Hallow. I hope June didn't think I forgot about her."

"No, she didn't." He got out of bed to put a spoonful of coffee in her mug. "I explained to her that my DVD collection exposed me for what I really am—a vampire fanatic."

She shuffled back and leaned against his headboard. "You're making that coffee like you've done it before. Maybe you really are just a fanatic."

"Maybe I am. Would that be easier for you to deal with if I were?"

"Ironically, no, it wouldn't." She was about to say something then paused.

"Don't be shy. Speak your mind," he said as he poured the milk in.

"Okay. Will you be joining me for a drink?"

He frowned. "You want me to have a coffee with you? I can if you want me to?"

"No, that's not what I meant." She took the coffee from him when he handed it to her.

"You mean blood. I have already fed. I didn't think you would be ready to see me do that yet."

Maybe he was right, and yet she felt she had to see it to fully believe it. "What's the time?"

He checked his phone. "Nine-fifteen in the evening." When she groaned, he quickly added, "It's a full moon tonight, and the landscape couldn't be more stunning."

Another phrase of hers.

"I'll take this coffee up with me, have a quick shower, then I'll be right back down with my supplies."

"Or, you could take your time drinking your coffee, then allow me to take my time with you in the shower, and then go upstairs to collect your art supplies."

She sipped her coffee. "Your plan definitely sounds better than mine. I wonder why you said it, though. Do you think that humans subconsciously buzz around because our time is short? And you don't because you have all the time in the world?"

He had an odd mixture of shock and amusement in his eyes, then he lifted her top lip up.

She spluttered. "What are you doing?"

"I was just checking that *you're* not a vampire."

Chapter Twelve

It took little to convince Theodore to have a shower in her bathroom instead of his. His need to please her was more peculiar to her than what he was. So there was no need for her to persuade him by asking him if he had seen it since Bill put all the plants in there, creating a tropical haven. And although it had felt strange leading him up the stairs to show him a room in his own house, she had felt excited. Watching his eyes light up had been worth it.

"Thanks to the moonlight streaming through, we don't even need to turn the lights on. Isn't it exquisite?"

He answered her by pulling his hoodie she wore up and over her head, leaving her breasts bare to him. "Yes, exquisite."

Molly had never felt so desired, and it gave her a confidence she never knew she had. Sitting on the edge of the claw-foot tub, she said, "I have a confession, if you'd like to hear it?"

"Are you going to confess to covering all the cameras up here with pink socks?" He pointed towards the ceiling through the open door.

She giggled, then turned on the tap. "It would seem that I have two confessions. The second is that I fantasised about you in this bath after I met you. Even though our first introduction was humiliating."

"The fault was mine, not yours. Tell me what you fantasised about, and I will make it up to you by making it a reality."

"You did make it up to me." She poured bath salts in. "I thought of you in here with me, washing each other, then kissing each other until I couldn't wait any longer. I then wrapped my legs around your lap and made love to you, not caring when the water splashed over the sides."

Theodore slid her bottoms down, and then she unbuttoned his shirt and slid his bottoms down before they got in the bath. While they were living out her fantasy, his fangs scraped her neck, sending chills throughout her body before she came. When he joined her, he shuddered and pushed himself in as far as he could. Afterwards, she turned around and leaned back against his chest.

"We missed the part where we washed each other first." He massaged her shoulders. "Shall we start again from the beginning?"

* * *

As much as Molly enjoyed wearing Theodore's clothes, she was glad to be wearing her skinny jeans and tight jumper she wore while painting. The once black outfit was now multicoloured, covered in a buildup of paint after years of her smearing paint on them from her fingers. And the reason she was glad to be back in them was because she needed a reality check. Being with Theodore was everything she had ever wanted and more, but she needed to keep her feet on the ground. They barely knew each other—not really. Not to mention he was an entirely different species to her. Did it matter? She guessed it didn't. Especially when they were together, enjoying each other's bodies. And it wasn't as he left Molly with a feeling of wanting more than sex. It felt to her like they had skipped months of getting to know one another by going on dates and entered a relationship. If that was the case, then she needed to know what being a vampire really meant. Because when he ran his fangs over her skin, she knew she wouldn't have denied him if he wanted to pierce her flesh, and it scared her. She would never allow herself to feel used again—ever. So she needed to uncover whether blood sharing was their version of a shared kiss, or if she'd just be his own personal blood bag.

"Why are you frowning? Are you upset by something?" Theodore asked after he shut the back door. They were going to find the perfect spot for her to paint while he read through some paperwork that was sent to him to prepare for the next council meeting in three night's time.

"What would it feel like if you were to bite me?"

"It would hurt you, and I would never do it. Even if you wanted me to. As you already know, we created many of the vampire films, but the films that depicted vampires taking blood from humans as a sensual act were not. Although it is sensual between two vampires."

Molly smiled at that, and that was why she needed to know everything. She didn't want to jump into the deep end with a blindfold on, but at the same time, she didn't want her jaded past to put up unnecessary barriers between them. "That's not really what I wanted, but when we're together, I feel like I could never deny you."

"You'll have to trust that I have your best interests at heart and would never hurt you." He put his paperwork down on the garden table and propped her easel against it, then held her face in his hands. "And know that I could never deny you, either. You are mine now, and your happiness is my priority."

"You said taking blood is a sensual act between two vampires. Wouldn't you feel like you'd be missing out?"

"Some couples don't hold hands in public—some do. Some couples don't cuddle in bed—we do." His grin made her heart pound. "Every couple is different. There is no right or wrong way."

Molly stepped back. "Do you think we've rushed into this? Shouldn't we take things much slower?"

"Why?" He put his hand on her lower back and pulled her towards him. "Because your society dictates that we should take things slow?"

"'*Your society'*. See what I mean? It's not just a case of us getting to know each other, it's also about getting to know..." She spun her finger in the air, trying to think of the right words. "Each other's differences."

"I may have closed myself off from the world, but I understand human nature very well. I hope, in time, you'll see that the vampire way is much less complicated."

She balanced on her tiptoes to kiss him. "The fewer complications, the better, but will you meet me in the middle until I fully understand your ways? Also, I think I'm still in shock. I seem to forget what I've learned about you. Then when you smile or when the light catches your eyes in the dark and they glow green like a tiger's caught on an infrared camera, I'm reminded of what you are. It's like you're not even real—in more ways other than the most obvious. And I'm okay with it. It's just an adjustment, that's all."

"I understand."

"You do?" She tilted her head to the side.

"When I look at you, I can't believe you're real, either. I have waited so long for you, Molly."

Wanting to say something in return, something as open and honest as his declaration, she was about to speak her mind, but she didn't have the courage to say the words. When he said things like that, it was hard for her to not jump in at the deep end into the unknown. Which could lead to her getting hurt. However, when she looked into his eyes, all she saw was a future that promised fulfilment, happiness and untold pleasure. And yet. "Shall we see if the lake has the reflection of the moon in it? It should sell shortly after I've listed it on my website because my winter and night pieces always go first."

There was amusement in his expression. "Very well. I know what will please your human complexities. Why don't I introduce you to my parents before we go to the lake?"

Molly giggled in hand. "At least their headstones can't disapprove of me, and neither can mine."

"How macabre of you." He laughed before putting his paperwork and her easel under his arm and taking her hand with his other. "Follow me."

The graveyard was dreamlike, with no breeze, and the temperature only having a slight bite to it, making Molly feel like she was walking on air. Not to mention the way Theodore walked before her. He walked with purpose, whereas she could only see what the moon illuminated, making her walk with caution.

"This is my uncle." His voice was gentle. "It's very rare for a mated pair to have more than one offspring."

Mated pair. Offspring.

However, it wasn't his choice of words that reminded her of what he was; it was the dates carved into his uncle's headstone. "He was three-hundred and… Maths isn't my strong-suit."

"Three-hundred and forty-seven. He was young and hadn't found his bride, so I mourn for him the most."

"Young! That's a long time to be without a partner. Assuming that's what you meant when you said bride. What's the difference between a mated pair and being a bride?"

"A bride is a mated female."

"Do vampires marry, or does being mated mean the same thing?"

"Finding your fated mate is so much more than marriage because we mate for life."

"Vampires mate for life?"

"Is that something you would want? To be married for life?"

He looked at her, as if he was trying to read her mind, and she knew she'd have to choose her words carefully. "I was living day to day with only one goal, so I had put little thought into it." When he looked disappointed, she added, "But I liked the idea of finding someone after I achieved my goals, and marriage would certainly be a bonus. If he was the right man."

"Or male." He grinned. "My mother and father are over here."

As she followed him to the largest of the headstone, she realised it was a double grave. She traced her hand over the engraved marble. "They died in the same year."

"Five days apart. Like I said, vampires' mate for life. If one dies, the other follows. The loss is so great, the heart just stops beating. It's a human phenomenon, too."

"I have heard about that. Still, it's hard to imagine, and I have felt a significant loss before. I just remembered something. June and Bill said you never left the house. Does it feel strange to you being out here?"

He took her hand. "I took your biscuits to Bill because I didn't want you to find them untouched and feel upset by it, and being outside for the first time in years felt strange. That being said, tonight, it just feels right. I'm looking forward to working outside while you create your next masterpiece, and, of course, spending time with you." He kissed her hand. "And I'm glad you've chosen the lake. I have missed it."

Instead of tentatively placing a foot in front of the other while she walked through the small wooded area, she followed Theodore, knowing he wouldn't let her trip and fall. Proving her point, he stopped, faced her, and guided her down a couple of steps she wouldn't have seen. When they came to a clearing, and the lake came into view with the moonlight bouncing off it, she felt a thrum of excitement. "Perfect. Can we stop here?"

He opened her easel for her. "You set up and I'll go back up to get the table and chairs."

"Okay." She pulled a clip-on torch from her bag, turned it on, and then clipped it and a blank canvas to her easel.

As she pulled out a pencil, a thought came to her, and she couldn't decipher it, leading her to feel confused. She rewound back to what she knew, and yet the results were the same. Why would Theodore lead her into a relationship that could never work between them? Was she just to be his entertainment until he found his bride? A female vampire that never aged and could give him—in his words—offspring. She wanted to ask him, but if she did, would she come off sounding needy?

"What are you thinking about?" He had already set up his table behind her.

"I didn't hear you walking back." She briefly turned to him, but couldn't look at him for much longer than that.

She felt his heat behind her before he placed his hands on her hips, then turned her to face him. "Tell me what is on your mind, Molly."

Knowing he wouldn't give in until she told him, and wanting to get it off her chest more so than coming across as needy, she didn't hold back. "Vampires mate for life, meaning we can't because I age and you don't, and yet you're not behaving like we're just having a casual fling. And I know it seems like a heavy conversation to have, considering its early days, but—"

"You should always voice any concerns you may have. Regardless of whether society tells you its early days."

She defended her point. "But it is early days. What if you decided next week that you didn't want to be with me? I would have to leave and would lose my job. I'd never see June and Bill again. What about Hallow?"

"That would never happen. I promise."

"You don't know that. What if *I* decided I didn't want to be with you? Or what would happen to me if you found your bride? My feelings for you are already strong, when they shouldn't be because *it is too early,* and I couldn't be around you while you were in love with another woman—female. Which sounds ridiculous, even to me." She looked away, not wanting to hear his words, let alone see them come from his mouth.

"Look at me." He brushed his fingers through her hair. "It pleases me to hear you say you have strong feelings for me, and it's never too early. Haven't you heard of love at first sight? I know that you have, and I bet you experienced it when you met Hallow for the first time."

"I did fall in love with her at first sight, but with people, it's different."

"Why is it?"

"It just is. And it doesn't really matter anyway, because I could never be your bride."

He took both of her hands in his and got down on one knee. When he looked up at her, she sensed his openness. "You are my bride."

His words rang true.

Chapter Thirteen

Molly blinked, opened her mouth, then closed it.

"That's impossible. You said… you said…"

He stood. "I didn't want to admit it to myself at first, believing it would be too complicated for you. However, it's not unheard of—for a vampire to fall for a human. We can make it work. We are making it work."

No longer in the mood to paint, she switched off the torch clipped onto her easel. She felt silly for what she was about to say—because it was too soon. And yet she knew it was only her that felt that way. So, she spoke freely. "You said, vampires' mate for life, and that I wouldn't have to worry about getting pregnant because it was impossible. If I'm your bride, we can't start a family—if that's something you wanted. And I will grow old. And you will, what? Die after I do? I don't want that for you."

"Molly, people grow old together. Look at June and Bill. They've been married for forty years. June is also proof that we can adopt. Say the word, and I will get you a baby."

She cupped her hand over her mouth before she laughed and then stepped into his arms. "I know people grow old together, but you're not *people*. You just proved it by saying you'd '*get me a baby*'."

Breathing in her scent from the top of her head, he said, "How would you have preferred me to say this?"

She thought about it, and although he sometimes sounded abrupt, she was soon becoming appreciative of it and his honesty. Being able to speak your mind without self doubt was a gift, and she was learning from him fast. "Okay, picture this: I'm eighty years old and I can no longer walk to the bathroom to wash myself or go to the toilet. Then what? Won't you regret not waiting for a vampire bride instead of a subpar human one?"

He switched the torch back on. "People grow old together every day and look after each other. Again, look at June and bill. She will have to help him get dressed and do many other things for him while he recovers. That's love. I have chosen a human bride, and there is nothing subpar about her. She, you, are more than I ever could have wished for."

She switched her light back off. "How about this, then? I'm eighty years old? My boobs are to my ankles and I've lost all my teeth, and every time I chew my food, my dentures fall out. You, on the other hand, will still look like a Greek god statue."

He flipped her light back on. "You think I look like a Greek god?"

"I'm trying to have a serious conversation, Theodore." She wrenched the light off the canvas and launched it as far as her strength would allow. "I will grow old and you won't. Therefore, we can not grow old together."

"Just because my appearance won't change, it doesn't mean we can't grow old together." The torch was only a few metres away, so it didn't take him long to retrieve it and put it back on the easel.

"Don't you want more?" she said.

"I have more than I ever could have asked for. I told you this. There will be no convincing me otherwise. Now, I was looking forward to doing some paperwork while you painted. Will you do this for me?"

Molly looked up at the stars, and then at the moon, hoping to find the answers, but they were silent. Perhaps if she painted, it would clear her mind and she could think clearly. "Alright, I'll drop it for now and paint. Maybe once I've spoken to June about it, it will help me understand and decide what to do."

At that, he smirked, then took his seat at the table. It's then that she knew June would be on his side, anyway. Still, it would help her to… wait! He wasn't smirking because of that, or rather just because of that. He was smirking because she said that after she spoke to June, she'd decide what to do. As if there wasn't a decision to be made because he'd already made it for them. While his head was down, she threw her pencil at his paperwork.

His grin was wide and unapologetic. “My new bride is feisty. I like that. Keep going and I will tear those jeans off you and take you over this table.”

“Ha!” She’d finally found an angle he couldn’t squirm out of. “Picture this: I’m eighty years old. Now I want you to imagine taking me over that table.”

His face dropped.

* * *

There was no use in begging the moon to stop moving while she sketched its outline. Similar to that of Theodore, the moon had a destination in mind and would not be detoured from achieving it. His counter-argument was that she was being ageist and that it didn’t matter how old you were or looked: passion was passion when you were in love. And if truth be told, she was glad Theodore would always win the argument in defence of their relationship; she didn’t want to lose him.

When the time came, maybe ten or twenty years from now, she would leave him for his own well-being. She shook her head and couldn't believe she found herself looking that far ahead. A lot could change from now until then. Yet, if she were to leave him, would that count as her dying? Would it cut his life even shorter than it already would be?

She turned to him. “And vampires still die even if their bride is human? Oh, you're squinting.” She looked over at the horizon and saw light threatening to spill over the landscape. “Let's get back inside. I need to check on Hallow and feed her, anyway.”

He looked at her with curved lips while he piled up his paperwork. “She’ll know doubt be in the same condition as the last four times you checked on her.”

She folded her easel. “I know, but it feels like I haven’t given her much attention since you got her for me.”

“Come on then, let's see if she’ll sit with us while we watch a film.”

“Ah, well, I thought I should probably get some sleep. I’m not a night owl, remember?” Although, it would go a long way in making her feel like she was in a normal relationship if they did something as simple as lounging in front of the TV. “Actually, watching a film does sound great, and then I’ll be up to phone June and see how she’s getting on with Bill.”

They began their walk back to the house. “Any film in mind?” he asked.

“Hmm, a werewolf one, I think. Just so you can bring me back to earth by telling me they don’t exist.” She laughed, and when he didn’t respond, she dropped her easel. “Theodore?”

He bent down to retrieve her easel. “You are clumsy, my love.”

She snatched it from him. “No, I am not clumsy. If I ask you about werewolves, are you going to tell me they are real? Because if you do, I won’t be able to sleep until you give me every detail, and I don’t think I can handle much more.”

“Then either don’t ask me—which would be impossible for you—or tell me not to answer your question as to whether or not they are real until tomorrow."

She put the easel under her arm and used the other to rub her temple. "Okay, this is the plan: I'll make a coffee, drink it, then phone June. After that, you can launch me into the deep end by telling me about every mythical creature ever known. Deal?"

As soon as he opened the back door that led into the kitchen, Hallow tried to get out. Theodore caught her in one arm and then cradled her to his chest. "Deal. Although, some will need explaining in depth. For example, some mythical creatures, as you put it, are in the form of everyday animals. Hallow, here, is an angel of death. When cats sleep, they travel to the realm between life and death, to ferry people's souls to their last resting place, wherever that may be."

Molly took Hallow from him and cradled her as he had done. "Well, that's not too scary, I guess. So, the Grim Reaper is a cat?"

Theodore flipped on the kettle for her. "I can't tell you how pleased I am. You were born for my world. And you are right; the Grim Reaper is a cat, or rather, all cats are the Grim Reaper."

She put Hallow on the kitchen side and looked at her. "So when I die, I'll see a cat?"

"I don't know about that because I don't know what the soul sees after it leaves the body. However, people with second sight say they see many cats in hospitals and places of war. Which would mean a cat can sense when a soul is close to leaving the body."

Knowing that a cat would one day guide her to her resting place, strangely, brought her some comfort. "I'm purposely not asking you about people with second sight because I want to drink my coffee and speak to June first, but why doesn't everyone know cats are angels of death? It would go a long way in helping people with the grieving process, knowing that their loved one wasn't alone when they pass away."

He pulled two mugs from the cupboard, and it pleased her because it meant he wanted to join her for a coffee to help her feel at ease. "You don't have to do that," she said. "That ship has sailed, so to speak."

"I want to. As for people not knowing about cats, there once was a time when they did. The people of Ancient Egypt worshipped cats for that very reason, but as the world moved forward, facts became fiction when they couldn't be proved otherwise. The only thing people worship now is science."

Molly followed him into the living room while he carried the mugs. "You sound disheartened by this. Is it because you've been relegated to nothing more than a myth?"

They sat, and he handed her a coffee, then he shuffled back on the sofa, pulled his knee up and then rested his elbow on it. Molly noted this because he didn't look like a seven-hundred-year-old vampire lord at all. His actions made him look more like a laid back thirty-something-year-old, and always would. Which made her feel validated in her argument against this relationship.

"Partly," he said, snapping her out of her thoughts and bringing her back to her surroundings. "Tell me what's on your mind, Molly."

There was no use telling him what she was thinking, which was her as an elderly lady, curled up against him while he sat like that, because he'd only have a counter-argument. Also, if he was willing to drink coffee with her, she bet he'd be willing to not sit like that as well, to make her feel more comfortable around him. And there was another reason; she was as greedy for him as he was for her. She would do her best to convince herself to not worry about the future, and to enjoy her time with him instead. Yet, she knew she would fail. How could she not? Her eyes watered.

Concern for her was etched in Theodore's expression before his phone rang, saving her from having to explain herself. "Is that June?" she said.

He nodded, then handed his phone to her.

"Hi, June. It's Molly."

"Good morning, my dear. You're up early, or shall I say, late?"

Hearing June's voice was exactly what she needed. "The latter. How is Bill getting on?"

"He's doing so well. The doctors have had him up and about already, and they think he'll be better than before."

"Oh, I'm so pleased, June. I'm surprised they've had him up and about, though."

"So was I, but it's protocol now, so he doesn't stiffen up and lose muscle mass. Anyway, enough about us. Aren't you a smarty pants, unearthing the secrets of an ancient immortal by his bloody DVD collection?"

Molly laughed, not only at what she said, but at how she said it, making her miss June even more than she did. "And what you and Bill had said. I remember on my second day, you almost called him a vampire. Not that I would have put two-and-two together back then."

"Back then? That was less than a week ago. I'm proud of you for not doing a runner, and I'm pleased as well because it means I won the bet I made with Bill. He thought you'd do a runner, then come back when you had time to adjust."

She looked over at Theodore, and her heart skipped a beat. His smile really was devastating. "I just found out that cats are angels of death, and I'm about to learn whether werewolves are real. So tell Bill he hasn't lost the bet yet."

June laughed. "The wolves are nothing to fear, and unlike what you've heard, they just look like regular wolves and only take human form when it's a full moon. They mainly live in Canada now and are protected by the vampire council."

Whiplash was something Molly had never experienced before, and yet she was certain her mind had just jerked forward and backwards with such force, it caused a flash headache. "Umm…"

Initially, there was silence on June's end, and then she said, "It must be love if my father isn't reprimanding you for using improper words."

My father.

"Umm..." Improper word or not, she was lucky enough to even muster that. Thinking you had accepted one thing, only to have it confirmed after learning that cats and Canadian wolves are things of legends, was now causing her headache to spread to every curvature of her skull.

Theodore reached over and took the phone off her.

"That's enough information for her for one day. Will you give Bill my best?" He listened to June's response, then said, "I love you too. Bye."

Then he put his phone on the coffee table before sitting beside Molly so he could put his arm around her. "Why don't we go downstairs so you can sleep?"

She snuggled into his chest. "Mermaids?"

"Has your mind completely scrambled, and that's now your new word for yes?"

"What? No. Mermaids, are they real or not? I want to know because I've always wondered how they went to the toilet."

He laughed, then sighed. "I truly believe you need to sleep to give your mind a break."

"Or, you could tell me everything, so I can sleep on it."

"Only if you're sure. Stop me if it gets too much for you, okay?"

She nodded.

"First, sit on the floor between my feet, and I will massage your shoulders while I tell you. It will help keep your stress levels down."

Never having a massage before, Molly obliged him without question. When he kneaded her neck and shoulders, she felt as if he could tell her the world was about to end and she wouldn't care.

"To my knowledge, mermaids have never existed, but I like to keep an open mind and say, they could have existed thousands of years ago."

His answer was comforting. Not just because he said they didn't exist, but because, like her, he still left a bit to the imagination.

"Dragons?"

"Extinct."

Her eyes widened. "That's a shame. When and why did they become extinct?"

"The same reason the dinosaurs went extinct. Although, we're not entirely certain how that happened other than an asteroid hitting earth, triggering a tidal wave of events."

She sighed a sigh of relief and then felt stupid for overthinking things. "They were just dinosaurs, then?"

"The most magnificent of them all, I should imagine. You seem disappointed."

"No, I just feel that perhaps I've opened my mind up too much. It would appear that there's a reasonable explanation for all mythical creatures."

"Do you mean, like wolves turning into humans when it's a full moon? Oh, okay," he said, with uncharacteristic sarcasm.

Molly giggled. "'Oh' is not a word, Mr Ardelean."

"It's a valid scrabble word. Call me Mr Ardelean again. I like it."

"Mr Ardelean, tell me about witches and wizards."

“That will need a detailed explanation. There is magic in the world, and we, as well as humans, can harness it.”

“Okay, we’ll come back to that one. How about demons?” At that, his hands stopped massaging her. She turned and saw sorrow in his eyes. “Hey, what is it?”

Just as it looked like he wouldn’t answer, he said, “It was a demon who took my father’s life—and my then my mother’s five days after he died.”

Chapter Fourteen

Molly wanted to spare Theodore the pain of talking about his father's death by telling him he didn't have to tell her, but he spoke before she could.

"Demons are not really demons at all. They are spiteful fallen angels, bitter and twisted, and are never content with people wanting to live their lives as they see fit." There was venom in his voice, and rightly so.

"Other than cats being angels of death, actual white-winged angels exist?" she murmured, as her mind expanded even more than it had to accept what he'd said.

"The angels of death have a purpose. Those white-winged fuckers are pointless creatures. They're supposed to keep the scales of good and evil balanced. How you do that by observing and not intervening, I'll never know."

"You don't have to go on if it's hard for you." She faked a yawn. "I could sleep now. Shall we go to bed?"

The affection in his eyes for her was almost too much to bear. Other than her parents, no one had ever loved her before, at least not to her knowledge. If her grandparents felt that way, she'd never felt it from them. And it kept her awake a night with worry, thinking she'd never recognise it, if it ever was directed at her. Theodore wore his heart on his sleeve, leaving her without doubt, making her heart swell even more for him. It frightened her, and yet she wanted more—she wanted to give more of herself to him, too.

"Maybe it's for the best," he said. "After you've eaten something."

At that, her stomach rumbled. *Bloody hell,* she thought. Never had she missed a meal before. Or in this case—she counted in her mind—three meals. It must have been all the excitement of the recent discoveries. When she thought about what she'd eat, the thought of Theodore sitting opposite her without a plate came to mind.

"Hmm, would you mind giving me some privacy while I ate? It would feel as if you were watching me if you didn't, and after years of living by myself, I wouldn't know if I had terrible table manners or not."

He grinned. "Alright, I'll give you some privacy. Twenty minutes should be enough, agreed?"

Believing initially he was joking, she laughed.

Twenty minutes later, Molly shooed him out of the kitchen. He reluctantly obeyed. Then, since there wasn't a dining room, she took her cooked food into the office so she could eat at the desk. She had made herself cheese on burnt toast with beans and burnt mushrooms—her favourite, and if she were on death row, her chosen last meal. Yet, although her stomach had rumbled, she didn't have much of an appetite. While she chewed her food, she wondered what it would be like to be a vampire, never to consume food. Did they smell it the same way she did? If so, did the smell of food make their mouth water the same way it made hers? If she were a vampire, she didn't think she could pass up burnt toast—or burnt anything, for that matter. But then, if she were a vampire, she wouldn't know any different, would she?

Something within her tired mind was trying to come to the surface. What was it? She stopped chewing, closed her eyes, and let the thought come to her in its own time.

"Huh, I hadn't thought to ask him that." And yet, something told her, since he was so determined to 'grow old' with her, that he may hold back with some details if her suspicions were correct. Or maybe she was way off. Either way, she wanted to put her mind at rest.

So she picked up the phone and rang June. She answered on the third ring. "You're in luck. I just arrived at the hospital and I was just about to turn my phone off. Are you okay?"

"Just a quick question: can humans become vampires, or are they all born? Oh, I don't know. It's probably a stupid question, but I have seen it in films, and since it was vampires that created most of them, I just wondered if it was a possibility."

The silence Molly heard told her that June either wouldn't answer, or she was choosing her words before speaking them aloud. Her silence also answered her question, but she would hear what she had to say, including the details.

June cleared her throat. "You're an intelligent woman. That's why you're asking me instead of asking him. All I will say is that the library in the turret holds the answer to your question. Tell Theodore that you want to see inside. He will not deny you. As your male, he is compelled to obey you—"

"Compelled to obey me?"

"Yes. Molly, I have to go. Let me know how you get on. I really hope you make the right decision—for my father's sake—and for yours, of course."

"What decision?" she asked, but June had already put the phone down.

Hallow leapt onto the desk, making Molly jump, then she jumped again when she saw Theodore leaning on the door frame to her left.

His face was unreadable, and yet in between the lines, she concluded that he had heard the conversation. But how? "You have superb hearing, don't you?"

"I can hear a pin drop a mile away. So, are you going to ask me if you can see my mother's library?"

She wanted to, but after the conversation they'd almost had about his father's death, she didn't want to cause further upset, so she gave him an alternative. "How about this: you can either show me the library in your own time or you can just answer the question I asked June?"

He walked over to the desk and pulled out the chair opposite her. "A vampire can turn a human with their blood—with only one drop. It acts like a virus; attaching itself to healthy cells, destroying them, and then they multiply at a rapid rate before getting to work reconstructing your DNA. Your body won't be able to produce cells fast enough to fight off the virus, and it soon becomes the dominant strand."

"Sounds simple enough when you put it like that. What are you yet to tell me?"

"Most of the time, the virus kills the human host before they can fully transition. The host has to be female because they are built to withstand viruses more so than men—something mother nature put in place, along with giving women a higher pain threshold to support childbirth. And the host—the human has to be in pristine health."

"Is it something I would survive?" She could tell he didn't want to answer her.

"There's a high chance you would survive it, but I would never take that risk—ever! Do you understand?"

Molly nodded. "I understand."

* * *

It took some convincing, but the following night, Theodore agreed to give Molly some space. She was now in her private living quarters, doing the final touches to Bill's painting she had created for him. She also wanted to go to bed before midnight, wanting to wake up in the morning rather than at night.

She tutted when she saw it was already two in the morning and she wasn't the least bit tired. How fast she had adjusted, she'd never know. Although she did, didn't she? Even though it was hard for her to admit, she wanted to adjust to his schedule. Molly may have needed space, but knowing Theodore was downstairs and she could see him whenever she wanted, kept her in company with him.

Their relationship came at a high price to him. The price was a shortened life and something he was prepared to pay without question—for her. What sort of person would she be to allow that to happen? And yet, if she were to walk away now, it wouldn't make a difference. Or did he just say that to keep her with him? No. He wasn't like that.

For the first time, since she opened her heart to him, she felt dread seep into her heart. Which translated to the feel of being trapped. A different type of trapped than that of which she felt with James, but trapped all the same.

June's words came to mind. *'I really hope you make the right decision,'* she had said to her, as if she had one to make. But then, she did, did she not? Sort of, anyway. Knowing June for only a short amount of time, she knew June would not purposely put her in harm's way. Meaning, June knew she would survive the transition of becoming a vampire. Her love for her father, Theodore, also confirmed to her she knew she would survive it. That was the decision June was talking about—becoming a vampire to spare Theodore future anguish.

It would certainly solve the other issue she had about her having to grow old while he never looked a day older than the day they met, and of him counting down the days they had left together when she, over time, became a liability. Not that she would feel that way if it were the other way around. And yet, that was the problem, wasn't it? She could see it so clearly from his perspective, because she would do the same for him.

So if she would do the same for him if the shoe was on the other foot, why not make the ultimate sacrifice by becoming a vampire?

Like she had done many times in the past, she wrote a list of pros and cons in her head.

Cons: she would never feel the sun on her skin again and never eat her favourite foods. What else? She came up blank, then laughed at herself.

"What is it you find so amusing?" Theodore said.

She spun and saw that he was standing right behind her with a bottle of red wine and two glasses—one of which was already full. She noted that the bottle was yet to be opened. "You explained to me once why cats wore bells on their collars. I'm thinking you should wear one too. I know what is in your glass, and I hadn't thought to add it to my cons list."

"Cons list?" He settled on her sofa and put the bottle and glasses on her coffee table.

"Yeah, that's what I was laughing at before you came in. My ridiculously small cons list."

"Regarding?"

"I think you know. Anyway, I don't think I could consume blood—even if I were to pretend it was red wine."

He stood, stepped behind her, wrapped his arms around her, and then rested his chin on her shoulder to look at her canvas. “Bill is going to be so pleased by this. You’ve immortalised his art with your own.”

“I hope so.”

“Look at me.” She turned in his arms and wrapped hers around his neck. “I don’t mind you having a cons list; so long as the pros list remains even shorter.”

“What if that one pro trumps all the others?”

“Risking your life is the con that trumps all others. Come sit with me. The space you wanted from me has come to an end,” he said, then rolled up the edges of her jumper with a look of desire in his eyes.

She knew he was trying to manage her by using sex to change the subject, but she didn’t care. He could manage her all he wanted, because unbeknown to him, she could not be swayed from her train of thought. All he was doing was simply giving her a much needed break from it.

* * *

After another amazing night, filled with passion, Theodore watched Molly fall asleep to the melody of the birds chirping their morning song. His bride was highly intelligent, which pleased him. Perhaps she was so because she lived mostly inside her own head—like himself. However, it meant, coupled with her strength, that nothing could ever sway her. If she wasn’t a natural born creative, she'd make a fine detective, a lawyer, even a judge. She could be anything she wanted to be. Proving yet again that no matter what hand life dealt her, she was destined for success. And that was why he would never turn her life upside down. Yet, hadn't that already happened?

He frowned. Her world had been turned upside down, and yet she had taken everything he had told her in her stride. She didn't even treat Hallow any differently after discovering what she really was, nor had she overly reacted to him—not really, other than asking lots of questions. That, though, was part of her personality.

Other things about her became apparent. The way she adapted to the night in a matter of days. How she hadn't thought to eat until he reminded her to do so. How quickly she had waved goodbye to the restrictions of what human society deemed correct behaviour. And how she had become so confident in his presence, as if he made her feel at home and be herself.

He sat on the edge of her bed so he could look down at her sleeping form, so he could see her with fresh eyes. Then everything came into focus. She was a vampire in every way besides her DNA. Fate may have screwed them both, but he could never feel resentment; not after his uncle died before finding his bride.

Hallow leapt onto the bed and nestled beside Molly's shoulder. Theodore ran his fingers through her pelt and then went back in time to remember a conversation he'd had with his father.

Theodore had wondered how his father could risk his mother's life when the love between them was so apparent. His father had explained to him it was because he loved his mother so much that he had to, that she would have died if he hadn't. Not just because she was born to become a vampire, but because they had mated for life.

It was also the first time his father had explained to him why, when one dies, the other dies shortly after.

"When our kind mate for life, our love for one another isn't just an emotion, it's magic. We adapt to each other and our two hearts beat as one. When one half of your heart dies, the other is too weak to continue," His father had said. *"Not only did I know your mother would survive the transition, she was already half-way there."*

He remembered his father had said his mother couldn't keep down food and how the sun had started to irritate her eyes. Back then, he hadn't paid it much heed. Why would he have back then? It was not as if he had expected his bride to be a human, too. It was rare that it happened, even rarer for it to happen to both father and son. And that was why there wasn't much information on the subject—if any. Still, there was a council meeting due tonight. He would ask for the records on all mated vampires and see how many cases there were where one of them was once a human, and see if their accounts mirrored his fathers.

If there were similarities, what were his options? To tell her to leave? Breaking the bond between them before it developed any further.

"No, I can't do that," he whispered.

Molly stirred. And why wouldn't she? If everything his father had said was true, it would mean that her hearing was becoming stronger. It also meant it was too late to reverse what had been done.

Chapter Fifteen

Molly had just assumed she wouldn't be present for the council meeting scheduled for tonight—in less than an hour—so when Theodore said he wanted to show her his mother's library before they attended the meeting, she felt buzzed with excitement.

"Are you certain?" she asked while they were standing outside the door.

"There is something I need to ask my associates, and since you will be present, I wouldn't want you to feel blindsided." His forced smile was for her benefit, making her feel guilty for wanting to see what she was about to discover.

Taking a step back. "We don't have to, Theodore. If I'm blindsided, I will deal with it. After everything I've learned over the last few days, there isn't much else that could shock me, is there?"

This time, his smile was genuine. "I think this might."

It didn't happen often when the feeling of uncertainty overrode her curiosity, making it noteworthy and leaving her wondering why. Most likely it was because she was on cloud nine and didn't want to fall back down to earth. Not that Theodore could do anything to make her pause, she thought. "You could just tell me what's in there."

"Some things are easier to believe when you see it." A grin broke through his stoic expression. "I also want to see how long you take to work out what it is I want you to know."

"Really? The meeting starts soon."

"You better start now, then."

She tutted. "Unlock the door."

"It's never locked. Open it."

Looking from him to the door handle, she blushed. If she told him it was locked when she tried to open it so soon after she started, he would know she broke one of his rules. Or would have done if it was unlocked. Still, were they not past that now? "I have a confession."

"I wonder what it could be?" His tone was playful. "I don't believe you've been in there, so perhaps you thought I locked it because the door handle is stiff. Try again by putting a bit more weight on it."

The handle protested against her weight and then the door sounded like it was screaming when she pushed it forward. Dust and cobwebs were what she imagined would greet her first, but from what she could make out in the darkness, the library seemed immaculate. The sound of Theodore striking a match caught her off guard before she watched him walk around the circular room, lighting candles protruding from wall mounted candle stick holders. Her eyes ran up the rows of books until they disappeared into the shadows of the turret's highest point, and she wondered how his mother would have reached the books on the top shelf until she saw an old library ladder in the corner of her eye. Other than the ladder, there were two reading chairs and a small table.

Theodore sat in the chair without a word, or any indication of how he felt. So she walked over to him and ran her fingers through his hair, wanting to comfort him. "Are you okay? We can leave."

He took her other hand and laid a tender kiss in her palm. "Being in here used to remind me of my loss and how lonely I was. Being in here now, with you, fills me with warmth."

Feeling sheepish because she couldn't find the same heartfelt words to respond to him, she was glad when he continued. Even if it was to tease her.

"Come on, Detective Molly. You don't have long."

"Hmm." She looked around the library again. "Only four pieces of furniture. Candles are candles. You don't expect me to read these books, and judging from the language on most of the spines, I wouldn't be able to, anyway."

He answered her with a grin and a shrug.

"That leaves the framed photos in front of the books." At first, she looked at them without looking at who was in them and she hadn't seen such small oil paintings. "The same artist has painted them all. Am I right?"

"They are by the same artist," he agreed.

“The artist is a vampire because they were painted years apart. Judging from the clothes I see, many years between these two, I think.” She pointed to two in particular. “But that’s not what you wanted me to discover.”

Then she looked at who was in them. “You look just like your father. Is this your mother?”

When he nodded, she closed her eyes and tried to imagine Theodore's parents sitting in here. Two ancient beings who had something between them she and Theodore were in the early stages of having. It was a beautiful image, so she burned it into her memory.

“You are in a lot of these, in various stages of growth. You were a cute kid, but I can’t imagine you being one. If you know what I mean?”

He snorted. “No, I don’t.”

“Perhaps it’s because I can’t imagine what a vampire kid would be like.”

“Why not?”

Sidestepping, she said, “Do they drink blood from a certain age? Would your parents have said something along the lines of: drink all your blood or go to bed early?”

Molly couldn’t hear his laugh enough—even if it was at her expense.

“We are born with fangs and drink blood from our parents from birth. My mother or father would cut their thumb or finger on my tooth, allowing me to drink. How does that information make you feel? It would sicken most humans.”

"It's not sickening at all. I also think it's nice that the father can feed their baby, too." Unable to keep her emotions in check, she sighed a sigh of defeat. Even though he said he would 'get her a baby' if she wanted one, there was an image in her mind of him feeding their baby—with his blood. An image she no longer wanted in her mind, because what accompanied that image was a sense of longing.

"Molly, are you alright?"

"I am." She walked across the room and pointed to another. "Is this your uncle?"

"It is."

"Besides your parents, uncle and you, after hitting maturity, the people in the paintings age throughout them, and they don't have vibrant blue eyes. They were human, but who were they to you? In this picture, I would assume they were your grandparents, but how could they have been?"

"How indeed?" Pride filled his eyes, making her blush.

Knowing how fragile these paintings were, she hadn't touched them, but one in particular she wanted to see in as much light as possible. She looked over at Theodore for his permission before picking one up and walking closer to a candle. Then when she saw it, she couldn't unsee it. How could she not?

"Do all vampires have bright blue eyes?"

"Bright eyes, yes. The colour varies."

The two women in the painting, one of which was Theodore's mother, looked like mother and daughter. What had caught her attention was that in this one, his mother's eyes were an average blue. She didn't doubt for a second that this was a mistake by the artist. Which meant?

Molly put the frame back, then sat in the chair opposite Theodore. Bewilderment was an overstatement, but when Theodore pulled back his sleeve to see his watch before raising his brow, she giggled despite her latest discoveries.

"Eight minutes," he said. "I'm impressed."

"Why didn't you tell me your mother was a human?"

"It wasn't a secret. In any case, I'm sure June would have told you in time."

"You said you wouldn't put me at risk by…" She couldn't find the words. The prospect of changing from a human to a vampire was frightening—too frightening to even think about it. Not necessarily the process, more so because she would do it—for him.

He stood, then kneeling before her. "I would never put you at risk. However, I believe we have found ourselves cornered. You were right to feel uncertain about the complications our relationship may face."

What felt like a thousand thoughts rushed through her mind, most of which were causing anger to boil within her. Foolishness for her willingness to sacrifice her life as she knew it was at the forefront. Even if her willingness was born out of guilt for him having his life cut short, she should not have so readily submitted. "You've changed your mind about watching me grow old?"

"Never. Why would you think that?"

The look of certainty she saw in his eyes spoke volumes. The truth laid bare. She reached for her plait, only to find it was loose, then slammed her hand down on the arm of the chair. "I've always known my mind, and yet it feels like it's no longer mine, confusing me, making me feel like I don't know myself at all."

"Tell me. Just blurt it out. Let me help you."

Wanting space from Theodore to think straight, she stood. Then when she looked down at him, the thought of them being parted—even if it was just to the other side of the library—pinched at her heart. She groaned before sitting back down. "The truth of it is, I wanted to become a vampire to spare you. Just to spare you from having to worry, to having a shortened life. But I shouldn't feel that way. Why do I feel that way when, if you think about it, we barely know each other? And yeah, I know you said I'm your bride, that we're to spend our lives together, but why do I feel... Why do I feel..."

"Shh, shh. Don't cry." He stood her up to hold her while she wept tears of frustration, then continued. "Unlike a human, our love isn't fickle. It's an intense love, bound by magic, making it truly unconditional. That's why I said a mated pair is so much more than that of a human marriage."

"I understand that, but I'm a human. So why do I understand it? Why do I love you so much already? Why was I so willing to forfeit my life for yours?"

He picked her up, then sat down with her on his lap. "Hearing you say that, even under these circumstances, pleases me to the point where there aren't the words to describe how I feel. I love you, too. I will always love you."

Molly smiled despite still feeling confused. "Do I feel like this because you're the first person I have ever loved? I feel that there's more to it. Like there's an explanation."

"You are right to feel as you do. It has something to do with why I needed to tell you about my mother before the council meeting. Molly, I don't want to frighten you. However, I can't abandon you to your own thoughts, which would lead to more confusion. Which would lead to you feeling even more frightened."

At that moment, she didn't feel frightened. She felt that whatever she was about to learn; they'd overcome it. More blind trust, she thought. Although this time, after they'd confessed their love for one another, she welcomed it. "Tell me."

"You've only eaten once in the last few days. It's true that human eyes can adjust to the darkness, but you are seeing in the dark. Last night, when you drank the entire bottle of wine, you were not the least bit tipsy. Tell me something, my love. Were you just curious about the blood in my glass or did you hunger for it? When you bit my neck during sex, did you do that because you thought I would like it, or did you do it because it came natural to you?"

She hadn't given it much thought, not wanting to overthink things like she had been doing. The excuse she used for feeling thirsty when he drank blood from a wine glass was that she hadn't eaten enough. Why hadn't she asked herself why the sight of blood would give her a thirst, even if she was still hungry? Biting him was something she had put down to being in the moment. It was easier to believe that than the alternative. Which was a primal urge to consume his blood—to take more of him into herself. Why hadn't she asked herself why? Because it was too far-fetched. Impossible.

"Tell me. Say it aloud so I don't suffer a mental breakdown by trying to figure out the meaning of it all."

"Our love for one another. It's how I knew you loved me before you told me. You're adjusting to me. Vampires adjust to each other until their hearts beat as one."

"Are you saying I'm transitioning, anyway?"

"It's impossible. However, your human DNA is at war with your emotions. I'm worried about you. What if you no longer want to eat food or be in the sun? I once asked my father why he risked my mother's life. He told me he did it for her. That he had no choice."

"What are you saying? Will I die if I don't change?" He was about to respond, but she wasn't done. She needed to make sense of this information by speaking it aloud. "It's okay. We'll figure it out. I will need some time to think this through—by myself so I can think clearly. And if you think about it, it's easier like this. Having the situation decide for us rather than us deciding. We'll both get what we want. You won't have to watch me grow old, and I won't have to watch you watch me grow old."

“Molly, this isn’t what I want. I asked the council members to bring all or any information they have regarding this, to prevent this mid transition.”

“Why?” She stood. “Why stand in the way of the inevitable?”

“I will not risk losing you. You could have an underlying health issue. You could die.” He stood, towering over her, looking menacing, but she didn’t feel threatened. She felt his distress as if the emotion was coming from her.

Not wanting to fuel his despair, she chose not to argue her case further. It was a discussion that could wait until after the council meeting. Judging from the way things have gone so far, someone at the meeting may even throw another spanner into the works. Or ten more spanners. Maybe they’ll tell them that Theodore would start growing old. Who knows?

“What are you smiling at?” he asked, running his hand down the length of her hair.

Molly shrugged. “Do you have any idea what you’ll discover from the information? That’s if they have any.”

“I’m in the dark as much as you are.”

“Wouldn’t you say you understood more about the subject than them?” She stepped back and looked up at the books she could never read unless she learned the language. “Could some of these books be journals? Maybe your mother wrote about her experience. Before and after.”

"I believe you may be right, my love. Some of these are journals. I'll start reading them after the meeting."

"And you will share the information with me?"

He looked insulted. "Of course."

"Even if she's written about how she and your father were in the same situation as we are, and that she could no longer consume food. Theodore, yesterday, I was eating my favourite meal. Today, the thought of eating it makes me feel sick."

Chapter Sixteen

Telling him the thought of eating food made her feel ill, ensured her he wouldn't leave any details out. Not because she thought he would be dishonest, but because he wouldn't want her to worry. Something she would do, and therefore, something she couldn't be angry with him for. Also, they both needed to know everything, every detail, if they were to figure this out. However, if she could take back what she said to unsee that look of terror in his eyes, she would.

"I just heard the gates open," she said, sounding proud of the fact she had heard it from over a hundred metres away. "They're here."

This seemed to snap him out of his worrisome state. Now his demeanour was of determination, and Molly didn't know what was worse. At least it had overshadowed her nervousness over meeting other vampires. Now she only had a few minutes to deal with it.

"Are you nervous?"

“A little. A lot, actually. Only because I don’t know what to expect.”

“You’re not nervous because this could all be a ploy to lure you down below the basement so my associates can dine on you?” he said without a hint of humour.

“What? Why would you say that?” But she knew. He had said it to calm her nerves. As strange as it was, it worked. “You’re a wrong-en.”

His grin, as ever, was devastating. “And yet you love me, regardless.”

“Maybe I’m a wrong-en too.”

“No, you are perfect.” He kissed her hand and led her from the library down the hall. “Come on, let's get it over and done with.”

* * *

Bile rose from Molly’s stomach when the final vampire took her seat. There was hunger in all their eyes. Amusement, too. Hunger for gossip, she hoped, and not her. Amusement because they were about to banter with Theodore, and not because she had in fact been lured into this room to be dined on. She trusted Theodore, but seeing him among others of his kind… she just couldn’t describe how she felt.

What seemed like a lifetime ago, Theodore had commented on her lack of fear towards him, and she had said that perhaps if she had met a different vampire, she would be scared. Her assumption could not have been more accurate. Because even after knowing what she now knew, she was frightened. These vampires were frightening. The way they move like predators, stalking their prey. They were slick, gliding across the floor while they walked, then sitting in their chairs in one eerie, fluid movement. Their features were sharp, alluring, inviting. The clothes they wore screamed wealth and nobility. Their skin came in an assortment of shades, depending on where in the world they had flown from, and yet there was one commonality they all shared, which was that it was flawless—not even a freckle. How these vampires walk among humans, she would never know. And why hadn't she thought this way about Theodore? Well, she supposed she had, just not to this extent, because until now, it hadn't been this glaringly obvious. She dared a glance at Theodore, only to find him with his back to her while he spoke to the vampire to his right in a language she couldn't understand. She looked down and would keep her head down until this was over. Or not.

Molly couldn't help but look up when she heard the table being tapped. The vampire, the last to take her seat, was using her diamond ring as a gavel. When Theodore stopped talking, the vampire stood. "There is a human at this table. One that has only just discovered our existence. One that does not speak our languages. We will speak in her common tongue to make her feel more comfortable. We will apologise for not introducing ourselves." She pointedly glared at Theodore. "Even though her male should have done so the moment we entered the room. We will hope his bride knows enough to know we are solitary creatures, and that we lack social awareness—besides me—so that she is more likely to forgive us."

Theodore cleared his throat, faced Molly, and took her hand. "Please, forgive me." Then *he* pointedly glared at the female who had spoken. "I was waiting for everyone to arrive before making the introductions. You are late, Sophia."

She shrugged, dismissing him, then addressed Molly with one hell of a smirk. "At least you won't forget my name."

Molly liked her already. Not only was she more animated than the others, she broke the ice with ease, making her feel more comfortable. "You're right, I won't."

Theodore went around the table, introducing her to all the other members, one by one. He then ended the introduction by reminding her she had a lot of names to remember whereas they only had one, and told her not to worry if she forgot their names.

When the vampire, called Sebastian, opened his mouth, about to start the meeting, Sophia cut him off. "Oh, get on with it, Seb, or we'll be here all night."

Molly giggled, then sobered. She didn't dare look at Sebastian's reaction. Instead, she looked at Theodore, and was pleased to see he was smiling. When Sophia and the other's started bickering, Theodore whispered in her ear, "I'm truly sorry I didn't spot your discomfort. It won't happen again." Then he stood. "Enough," he barked.

Theodore motioned Sebastian to talk.

"First, I would like to congratulate Theodore and his new bride, Molly. And say what we're all thinking; The apple doesn't fall far from the tree." There were teasing cheers that followed, but to Molly, Theodore took it in his stride, and even looked proud. "Then I would like to discuss the recent restriction regarding hunting."

Groans followed that last statement.

Theodore turned to her while the debate was underway. "This conversation doesn't concern me. Would you like a coffee?"

"I'd rather you not leave me alone, thanks. When he said, hunting. He wasn't talking about animals, was he?" she whispered.

"No, he wasn't. He's talking about a law that was handed down four hundred years ago. The one I told you about, how only humans with a proven criminal record can be hunted."

"He said 'recent' restriction."

At first, Theodore looked blankly at her, then his lips curved. "Four hundred years ago, to us, is quite recent."

"Oh."

"The reason it doesn't concern me is that the law isn't within my jurisdiction. Also, no matter how much Sebastian harpers on, the law will not change."

"What is it he wants to change?"

"We only put known criminals on the list, people with a record of violence. Sebastian wants to hunt criminals unknown to the authorities. He believes the crime rate will lower at a much faster rate."

Still whispering, she said, "I understand."

Sebastian knocked on the table before standing. "Even Theodore's bride agrees with me—a human."

Molly inwardly cringed. Of course, he'd heard her whispering. "I understand your point of view, but there are criminals out there who are also victims. For example, some are forced into gangs through blackmail, fear, or some join to feed their families. How would you differentiate between the two types of criminal?"

"Very well said, Molly." Sebastian smiled at Theodore. "May I spar with your bride?"

"If you go easy. Remember, she's not a politician."

Her eyes went wide, the colour of embarrassment threatened to creep over her cheeks.

Sebastian looked her square in the eye—a male vampire who clearly advocated for hunting humans. "I agree with you. Some criminals are victims. Some people are forced into gangs to sell drugs, weapons or both. How about the people who are forced into gangs to sell people? Women—children. You know where I'm going with this."

Molly replayed his words in her head before responding. "For me, I'd rather die than inflict that type of pain on others. But would I feel differently if I had children to feed? I don't know the answer because I've never been in that position. How about targeting those who… buy services from these gangs instead?"

"I agree, it is a better alternative. However, some would say that those who 'buy services from these gangs' are unknowingly doing so."

"Not where children are concerned? Although, I have read stories about fake orphanages selling stolen children, but then, you wouldn't target a family bringing home a newborn baby, would you?"

"No. No one would. So you agree, people who hurt children and who are yet to get caught by the authorities should be fair game?"

Again, Molly replayed his words in her head. To her, people who hurt children were not people. They were monsters. She glanced at Theodore, hoping he wouldn't judge her answer too harshly.

"Pardon the pun," she said. Sebastian frowned at her, like she knew he would, making her smile. "They should be *fair game*—pardon the pun."

He slapped the table. "Next month, you're sitting on this side of the table with us."

Molly looked at Theodore for an explanation. "That side is pro hunt. This side is against hunting."

"Oh, I'm sorry. It is how I feel, though. Not that I could do it myself."

"It's okay. June's not a council member, however, when she's present, she sits on the pro hunt side."

"How is June?" Sophia asked. "Last we spoke, Bill had hurt his back."

Molly was grateful for the change of conversation and the mention of someone familiar.

"Bill has just had an operation. He's fine, and she's staying with him until he's discharged from the hospital."

"Excellent news. Talking of humans, you wanted information regarding Molly." Sophia smiled at her, acknowledging her, so that she felt included rather than the feeling she was being spoken about. "As you know, my mother was human. My father turned her without a second thought, making her healthier, stronger. I only know of you and your father who has ever resisted."

"Surely, there would have been others who feared for their mate's life," Theodore said.

"All vampires fear for their mates' lives. You're worried she wouldn't survive the transition. I understand that. But you know how fragile humans are. Molly could slip on ice, a step, a tennis ball. If she were to break her neck as a human, she may die. If she were a vampire, she'd stand back up as if it never happened."

"I would keep her safe." His tone was deadly.

"Keep her safe from fucking ice, steps and tennis balls?"

He stood. "No swearing at my table. And yes, I would keep her safe from all dangers."

"Theodore," Molly said. "Ice, steps and tennis balls aren't dangerous."

"Ice—"

"What are you going to do? Keep me locked in on icy mornings? I don't want that."

He looked defeated.

Sophia took a sip from her glass, then cleared her throat. "She's already adjusting to you, and if what you say is happening, she may starve—"

"There has to be another way. Someone other than me or my father must know something. Anyone?"

All the council members looked from one another, then shook their heads.

"Molly," Sophia said. "What do you want?"

"Do you all believe I would survive the transition?"

Every council member nodded their heads.

"The thought of eating food makes me feel ill. It could just be in my mind. Maybe I've just lost my appetite? Maybe I could force something down. But what if I can't, and I get sick? Would I then survive the transition?"

Sebastian answered. "It's a risk I wouldn't take. That being said, I believe this is cerebral. If you can't eat food, try drinking it. If it doesn't work, no more stalling."

"We only discovered this yesterday. Perhaps it is just a case of lost appetite," Theodore said.

"Theodore, if that is the case, with each year that passes, she'll become weaker—less likely to survive it. Why would you choose this?" Sebastian asked.

"I don't want her to suffer the pain of transitioning. She has a whole life ahead of her—as an artist. Above all, it's her decision. She may not want to be a vampire. It's too much to ask."

Sophia stood, then walked around the table to Theodore's side. "My mother said the pain was bearable. She said giving birth to me was far worse. So you can't use that as an excuse. Whether she's a human or vampire, she will still have her life ahead of her. She's an artist now—she will be an artist after. And yes, the decision is hers. Let her decide."

"She could have underlying health issues."

"I can hear her strong heart, smell her healthy blood. She has none. You're running out of excuses and running out of time. You have wanted her for years—wasting precious time. The next steps need to be discussed between you."

You have wanted her for years.

Molly frowned, turning that over in her mind. What did she mean by that? She glanced at Theodore. He looked sheepish, but was it because Sophia had won her argument, or because she'd said something which wasn't meant for her ears? Either way, she would find out why.

"Molly," Sebastian said. "What do you want?"

Theodore tapped the table to get his attention. "We'll discuss it in private."

In private, where he could try to convince her otherwise, and try to make her eat food. Then watch him panic if she can't eat it. Or watch him panic every time she slipped. Would he really try to keep her indoors if it were frosty outside? She loved him. She didn't want him to worry about her, but it would seem to her it was inevitable, whichever decision she made. And choosing to remain human may result in her resenting him if he over protected her.

She made her choice, and would say it aloud so she couldn't take it back, and she would say it in a room full of witnesses. "I will transition—"

Everyone spoke enthusiastically at once.

"Molly, we'll talk about it later."

"It's my decision, and I have decided this is what I want. I'm not saying I want to do it tonight, tomorrow or next week. I need time to accept the decision I've made—to decompress."

"This is excellent news," Sebastian said. "Molly, I will see you next month at the next council meeting—on my side of the table."

Molly grinned. "It was a pleasure to meet you, Sebastian. I will see you next month."

After each one of the council members bid farewell, and Sophia gave Molly a double air kiss, she and Theodore took their seats back at the table.

They both tried to speak at once. "You first," she said.

"Are you sure this is what you want?"

"It is. I don't want your life cut short, or for you to watch me decay—"

"Stop. I told you, you're more than I ever could have asked for. I would have you in any way I could."

"And that's why I want to do this. If you can make sacrifices for me, then why can't I for you? Although, after meeting more of your kind, it wouldn't be much of a sacrifice."

"You seemed to get on very well. I knew you would get on with Sophia."

"I was frightened at first—"

"For that, I'm eternally sorry."

"It's okay. But then, as the meeting went on, they all seemed quite open and honest, and I liked that. As for Sophia: it was nice to hear that you have something in common with her, and in a way, I do too. It kind of bridged the gap between us."

His eyes lit with amusement. "You would make a fine vampire."

"It's what you secretly wanted, isn't it?" she teased.

"What I want is to keep you safe, happy. To provide a life for you without pain."

"Pain is a part of life, and it makes you appreciate the good times. What did Sophia mean when she said you had wanted me for years?"

He accepted her admission with pride filled eyes, then said, "I've been watching you paint my house for years, admiring you."

"You're not an art collector, are you?"

He pulled her chair to his, then ran his hand up the inside of her thigh. "I am now."

She steadied his hand. "Did you ask June to employ me?"

"I did not. She did it in the hopes we'd wed one another, so that I wouldn't be alone after she and Bill..." He didn't want to finish his sentence and Molly couldn't blame him.

"I keep forgetting that in your eyes, we're married. Another reason why I need time in my own head to make sense of everything, to rewire my mind."

He kissed her. "Don't do too much rewiring. I just so happen to think you're perfect."

Molly kissed him back, deepening it, stirring the desire between them. He broke away, only to stand her up and lift her until she had her legs wrapped around his waist.

"You need to eat, if you can. I will cook you some burnt food—assuming that's how you like it, and not because you are a terrible cook."

She giggled, then unbuttoned his top button. "Before we head up to the kitchen, we could make a detour to your bed first?"

"Agreed. *Our* bed first, then food."

Chapter Seventeen

It was Theodore who had put a stop to Molly trying to force food down. Although her determination to try something rather than giving up at the first hurdle pleased him, watching her retch was too much for him to bear. It also drove home the facts; Molly would become a vampire. His vampire. His eternal bride. She had said it was what he secretly wanted, and she was right. What's more, she would still be an artist. She still had her life ahead of her. She would still become successful. Whether as an artist or whatever she wanted to be. As for the pain she would feel, it would be over in a matter of hours. If she went without food for much longer, her pain could last for days. So far, she said she didn't feel any discomfort, but that could soon change.

The countdown was underway.

"It's hard to believe that there are no records of this in our history," he said, thinking back to the meeting. As well as thinking back to how well she held herself—especially against Sebastian—who always had the last word. He suspected a friendship would form between them.

"There still could be in your mother's journals. We are now certain that we're not looking for a way out of this. Yes? But I believe we should still go through the journals, make notes, and create a file in case any future vampires end up in the same situation we've found ourselves," she said, leaning against the kitchen counter.

"You're thinking ahead. I like it. You will become an asset." He handed her a coffee. "Try this."

She sipped it without screwing her face up. "I can't taste the bitterness of coffee." She took another sip. "It's not as bland as water, either. More like a badly made cuppa."

"Badly made coffee or not, it's not making you feel sick. That's most important. Try this." He handed her a glass of water.

Again, she sipped it. "It's fine."

"Good. It buys us a little time."

She tilted her head. "But you want to get it over and done with now, don't you?"

Her inability to read his mind would never cease to amaze him. "The longer you go without food, the weaker you will become."

"That's true. But your mother and father have been through this, and they got through it. I will be okay. Shall we make a start in the library? You read—I take notes?"

"Sounds like a plan. Lead the way."

* * *

When they walked from the kitchen to the library, Molly felt like she was walking through the house for the first time. The artwork on the walls was for her. Theodore had turned his house into an art gallery for her. This house had also been her new beginning, a fresh start. Now she was entering another new beginning. An eternity with Theodore. She was nervous, excited, and like him, she was eager to get on with it now she had made her mind up. That being said, there was a part of her that wasn't quite ready to let go of the past without doing a few things first. Molly wanted to go back in time and tell herself that although a part of her life had been hard, she had made the most of it. She wanted to tell herself she was proud of herself, and she wanted to forgive herself for having the dark thoughts she had sometimes had. And there was only one place she wanted to do this. One place that felt right; her old flat.

The only thing that had stopped her from mentioning it was that she knew Theodore would not like it if she said she wanted to do this by herself. And she needed to be by herself when she did this. She wanted to speak to the framed photos of her parents alone. She wanted to be alone when she cried for her past, and she wanted to be by herself when she packed her remaining boxes of stuff.

So how and when would she tell him? His love for her was strong, as was hers for him. She would soon change for him—for herself. He would grant her this;

she would make him understand. Checking her watch, she thought, not without back-up. June should be awake in a few hours, and she would phone her if need be.

They entered the library, and both sighed before looking at each other, smiling.

“Where shall we start?”

“Knowing my mother, they will be in some sort of order. I’ll start in the middle.”

“Where’s the middle?” She walked over to a shelf filled with plain spined books. “Here looks like a good start.”

She pulled one out, opened it, and saw it was handwritten, then handed it to Theodore. “Each page has a date,” she said, knowing that would be all the help she could offer for now.

He read it, flipped another page, then sat down in one of the two chairs. “The date for this entry is two weeks before my father got murdered.”

Molly went to his side, not knowing how to comfort him other than to stroke his back. “I’m sorry, Theodore. We can do this another time.”

“No, it’s okay. It’s just that she’d written about such fond memories about my father, not knowing the end for them was near. It makes you think, doesn't it? How we should take nothing for granted.”

“If your mother was still writing fond memories after… How many years were they together?”

“A couple of decades before I was born.”

“Well, it sounds to me she never took him for granted.” She kissed his temple. His smile was weak, and he didn't respond before looking back over the pages. Her heart pounded, because depending on how often his mother wrote, he would soon come to the pages where she had lost her husband—his father. Not knowing what to do, she sidestepped. "Umm…"

He turned to take her hand. "I'm fine. It just feels strange revisiting the past under different circumstances."

"I can't imagine what you went through. To me, drink drivers are the lowest life form after one took my mum and dad from me. I'll never know how you got over…" Shit. Poor choice of words.

"I killed him. I ripped off his blackened wings, then twisted off his head. That's how." He stood before her, watching her, waiting for her reaction. There was regret in his eyes. Not for what he had done, she thought, but because of what she might think of him now. She didn't want to make him feel worse by saying the wrong thing, so instead she stumbled over her own tongue and asked him why the fallen angel had killed his father. As soon as the words rang out, she blushed.

"Just because he could, I think. That's what they are like. If not for my father's organisation, all vampires would have to hunt until another organisation was formed—something that took my father years to build. The fallen angel hadn't done his homework and didn't know about me. That much was apparent when I tracked him down. When I asked why he'd done it, he was half mad, repeating the same thing, over and over. He said, 'Let there be blood, death and destruction'."

"He was half mad, and by the sounds of it, he just wanted to cause mayhem between humans and vampires? I'm so sorry."

He nodded.

Molly closed the distance between them and held him as tight as she could. "These journals aren't going anywhere. Why don't we take the rest of the night off and watch a film?"

"Are you sure? The detective in you was eager to find out about the past so you could put a file together." He ran his finger from her temple to her chin.

"A mystery or thriller film will satisfy my inner detective. That's if you have any?"

* * *

This was the first time Molly had watched Theodore sleep. And she was in for a treat because Hallow had curled up in the crook of his neck. Her two most precious loved ones. Unable to sleep, for anxiety over—what she and Theodore had called—the next step, she crept out from beneath the blanket, and walked around his open living space. *Their open living space,* she inwardly smiled. She also couldn't sleep because she was yet to tell him she wanted time away in her own flat. But how could she, after what he had told her? And she could tell it was playing on his mind when they watched the film.

Not knowing what else to do, she headed to his office to answer some emails. To actually do something she originally came here to do—work. Wondering why he had so many screens when she sat at his desk, she turned on the one closest to her.

Every screen lit up simultaneously, momentarily blinding her. And yet, even through squinted eyes, she couldn't mistake what she saw. It was too familiar to be mistaken for anything else. But why? How? One screen showed her a shot of the high street she had worked in, the alleys she walked through to get to the art supply shop. Her bloody block of flats. "No. It can't be."

One angle was of the spot she chose when she painted his house. When he said he'd watched her for years, she had assumed he meant out of the window. She went back to the first screen, which showed the high street—which pointed directly at her previous place of work. Then, as she followed the screens from left to right, she saw how it covered her walk from her flat to work in order. Her suspicions were right—he had been spying on her. Although she never would have suspected he was to this extent.

Molly plonked into his chair and rested her head in her hands. How was she supposed to feel about this? Betrayed? Violated? She wasn't sure, but it was neither of those things. Instead, she felt… "Er. I don't know."

Flattered? No, no, no. Maybe. Yes. Either way, Theodore had crossed a line.

And this is exactly why she needed time alone to say goodbye to her past. It was the only way she could move forward with her new start. Checking the time, she saw that the sun wouldn't set for another couple of hours. Meaning; there wasn't a lot he could do about it after she left. Also, after what she'd just discovered, he didn't exactly have a leg to stand on, did he?

She ripped out a sheet of paper from his pad, then wrote him a letter.

Dear Theodore,

Stalking: when two people go for a romantic walk, and only one of them is aware of it. I'm not angry with you. Although I am angry at myself for not being angry at you. If you know what I mean. Anyway, I'm going back to my old flat to reflect and to say goodbye to my old life. I need to do this before I move forward. You'll know where I will be, since you already have my address. I'll be back in a few hours.

I love you, Molly xx

* * *

Theodore knew Molly wasn't in bed, even before he had opened his eyes. He slowly rolled to his side, to not wake Hallow with too much of a fright, then looked around, wondering where she could have got to. The lights were on in his office. *Not good,* he thought.

"Molly, my love?" he said, before entering. When he didn't see her, he scrambled to his desk to see if he could find her on the screens—which was no doubt the cause of her absence. Then he saw her letter, read it, then tapped away at his keyboard to show him a closeup of her flat. Close, but not close enough. A light was on, which meant she got there safely. He relaxed back in his chair, reread her letter in the hopes of it saying minutes, rather than hours, then smiled at her not-so-subtle way of calling him a stalker.

While he watched his screen, waiting for her to leave, he debated nipping out to get himself something to drink. As he stood, pulling his chair back, he saw someone at the front door of Molly's block of flats. Who was it? As he zoomed in, the image became blurry. However, there was no mistaking the person's silhouette. It was too distinctive to be anyone else's while she reached into her back pocket for her keys. The same way he had watched her do it time and time again.

If Molly had only just arrived, then who the hell was in her flat? There could only be one person.

His heart thumped. It would take him twenty minutes to run to her house. Fifteen minutes by the time he got his car from the garage and drove there. He hadn't driven anywhere in years. Where would he have left his keys? Fuck it! He'd have to run. Now!

Chapter Eighteen

Clearly, the locks had been changed for the communal door downstairs. Her annoyance was over in a matter of seconds because it wasn't like the landlord had any way of telling her. She purposely had given no one the details about where she would be.

Molly buzzed the doorbell for the neighbour who lived opposite her, hoping he would recognise her voice.

"Hello," he said through the speaker.

"Hi. It's Molly, your neighbour. It would seem the communal door's locks have been changed since I've been away. Could you let me in, please?"

"I assumed you moved out." He cut the line, then she heard the door buzz. Her cue that the door was now open.

After she closed the door and walked into the hallway, she wondered why her neighbour had assumed she had moved out when their paths had rarely crossed. Perhaps he saw the removal van.

She looked around the communal hallway, which seemed so familiar and unfamiliar to her at the same time. The artwork that decorated the walls of the staircases of Theodore's home was already sorely missed. And that was exactly what she had come here for, she supposed. To remember where she'd come from, and where she would spend the rest of her life.

As she walked up the stairs, she smelled smoke. Different. There wasn't a smoker in the building when she lived here. When she got to her top-floor flat, she frowned; the smell of smoke had got stronger. Wondering why her neighbour would have taken up smoking out of the blue, she fumbled with the lock, only to discover the door was already unlocked. How could she have left it open? She had never done that before. Even with the excitement she had felt that day when she moved, she knew she wouldn't have done that.

She stayed at the threshold and pushed the door forward. However, being in a flat meant the door was fire resistant and heavy duty, so it hadn't gone far before it swung back to close itself. Taking a step closer, she held the door a quarter way open. There was a light on. A light she knew she hadn't left on. And the smell of cigarette smoke and stale beer hit her senses.

James was here. Or had been here. He could have popped to the shops. He could come back at any moment. If he did, she would be cornered up here. With her hand on the handle, she crept back. Then the door flew inward, making her trip forward.

“You little whore,” James said, then grabbed a fist full of hair from the crown of her head.

A scream lodged in her throat. Her words of protest wouldn’t form.

He pulled her past the door, through her hallway, to the living room.

“No! Get off me.” Her fight or flight kicked in, making her claw at his fist, which still held onto her hair.

He let go, only to punch her square in the nose.

Before she felt searing pain, the crack of bone rang out in her ears. Blood poured from her nose and found its way into her mouth when she tried to take in a breath. But Molly couldn’t breathe. Her eyes bulged and her skin prickled. Like lightning, thoughts of Theodore, his gardens, and the time when she painted the full moon hanging over his lake, flashed through her mind. She needed to fight back. She needed to breathe, then fight her way out of this situation. A stream of oxygen made it to her lungs, then another.

“Where have you been, whore?” James was standing over her while she was on her side.

As she brought her knees up, she saw there was a look of excitement on his face. He was getting a kick out of her pain.

When she didn’t answer, because she couldn’t, he grabbed her by the ankles and dragged her across the floor before sitting on her. They fought when he tried to grab her wrists, so he punched her again—this time, splitting her lip. He then took her by the wrists and held them over head. In doing so, they were nose to nose.

"I said, where have you been?"

"Nowhere," she spluttered, spraying her blood over his face.

He twisted her wrist. "Where is nowhere?"

Her screams were weak, barely audible. Black dots swam around the perimeter of her vision. She was fading, passing out from fear and pain. He twisted her wrists again, waking her.

"He'll come," she said. "The sun is going down. He'll come for me."

If she ever, in the future, doubted Theodore, she would remember the certainty in her voice when she said that. He would come for her. However, the relief she felt was short-lived. He would come for her—only if he finds her letter in time.

Theodore crashed through his front door, only to be met with the setting sun. All he could see was white light, and yet, while blinded, he still ran toward the gate. A gate that could only be opened from the main house. When he crashed into it, he didn't even attempt to open it, instead; he ripped it off its hinges. After the metal screamed in protest and clattered to the ground, he went left, towards the town. A town he hadn't been to in decades, and had changed so drastically since then. A town he knew by heart because he had spent the last few years watching Molly walk through it.

"Who will come for you?" James screamed in her face. "Who?"

Molly didn't answer him. She needed to get out from underneath him, to fight him off and get out. She tried to buck him off, but he was too heavy. He laughed before putting more weight down on her wrists, keeping them in place, but she knew he would have to get off her, eventually. James would want to hurt her in other ways, and that was when she would make her move. He shifted her wrists on top of each other, then held them down with one hand. She slipped a hand away, only for him to slap her over her split lip.

When he held her down again with one hand, he reached into his pocket for something.

"Who will come for you? Your boyfriend?" He pushed down harder on her wrists. "Answer me!"

The sound of a spring mechanism snapping into place elevated Molly's heart rate even higher. It was the sound of a switchblade opening. Her head thrashed from side to side.

James held the knife to her temple, keeping her still. "Will your boyfriend still come for you when you're all carved up? Huh?" He pressed the knife into her skin. "Let's see, shall we?"

"No! Please. Don't do this."

He answered her by dragging the knife down from her temple, over her cheek. Warm blood spilled over her skin.

Theodore stopped, opened his eyes, only to see the outline of buildings. The sun had gone down.

However, his eyes were yet to adjust. Halfway there. Still too far away. Not knowing what to expect when he got there, he took out his phone to call Sebastian. He lived the closest to him—an hour away. But he couldn't see his screen. "Fuck!"

The roads were busy, so Theodore leapt onto the bonnets of the cars to cross to the other side. Horns blared, and he heard two cars collide before he turned into one of the many alleyways that led to Molly's flat.

Of all the pain she felt at that moment, it was her tears rolling over her cut that stung the most. James had got off her, knowing she couldn't move through shock and pain. Her hands trembled an inch from her face, wanting to touch it.

While she heard James banging open her kitchen drawers and rifling through them, a thought of him finding a bigger knife came to mind, giving her the strength she needed to roll over to her stomach. Her hair instantly stuck to her open wound, making her heave, and yet she pulled her knee up and attempted to stand.

"Just a thought." She heard James say before he yanked her back to the floor by her hair. "He might still be into you if you can cover your scar with your pretty long hair."

He stamped down on her stomach, winding her, then got back on top of her. When she got her breath back, she heard the gut wrenching sound of her hair crunching while it was being cut off.

When she tried to protect her hair with her hands, he either stabbed them with the scissors or cut her fingers. After he had cut off every stand, and her voice broke from screaming, he stood over her, looking frenzied, excited. "He definitely won't want you now. No one will."

She whimpered, running her bloodied fingers over her scalp. "No."

"Yes." He laughed, then pulled her hands away. "You look disgusting."

Knowing it wouldn't hurt him because she had little to no strength left, she kicked his knee.

His face dropped, then turned deadly before he reached into his pocket again. "You little bitch."

The fear she felt between him pulling the blade out, and the searing pain she felt when he plunged it into her side, was paralysing. It felt cold at first, then it burned.

Theodore shouldered the front door open and took the stair three steps at a time to the top. As soon as he got to Molly's front door, he smelled blood—a lot of blood. He opened it and followed the scent until he found her.

He was unsure whether his eyes were betraying him. Her hair was all over the floor. Blood stained the once cream carpet.

"Molly."

"He's still here." He followed her small voice to the corner of the living room, and saw her curled in a ball, squeezing herself against the wall. Her forearms were covering her face while her hands covered her roughly shown head.

"You're hurt. Let me see you." He tried to move her arms.

"No, don't look at me," she said, her tone pleading. "He's still here."

Theodore heard movement from the kitchen, which boiled his blood. The rage he had felt when he ripped off the fallen angel's wings paled in comparison. Knowing that the bastard couldn't get past him because the living room was between the kitchen and the front door, he took out his phone, called Sebastian, telling him to go to his house, then stalked from the room.

What he found was a pitiful human holding up a knife, trembling. No doubt from seeing Theodore's size, his strength, his fury.

"Move," the human said. "Move the fuck out of my way."

"You hurt my bride."

"Your what?" The human waved the knife back and forth, as if to remind Theodore he still had it.

Theodore's lips peeled back from his teeth, making the human drop the knife. "Pick it up." When the human didn't obey, Theodore bellowed. "*Pick. It. Up.*"

The human bent down to retrieve it, then stepped back as far as he could, against the kitchen worktop. "Stay back," he said, his voice as shaken as his demeanour.

"It's a crime to kill a human without a criminal record. Although exceptions are made for the likes of you." He stepped closer, the knife pressing against his abdomen.

When the human punctured his skin, and Theodore didn't react to it, he looked up. Fear and confusion seeped from his pores. "What are you?" He pulled the knife back, then attempted to stab him again.

Theodore grabbed the human's head in both hands. "The exception is that it's not a crime to kill a human who has hurt a vampire's bride."

His eyes widened before Theodore snapped his neck. When he turned to be by Molly's side, he heard the human's body fall to the floor with a thump.

Kneeling beside Molly, he tried again to move her arms out of the way to survey the damage. "Let me see."

"No." She fought against him, not wanting him to see her.

Her knees were to her chest, so he carefully tried to straighten one. When he did, blood gushed from an open wound under her rib cage. "He stabbed you."

Unsure whether or not it was fatal, he had to get her back to his home now for medical treatment. He scooped her up, then ran from her flat, only to realise he could end up causing more damage. Her arms, still tightly wrapped over her face and head, told him she still had some strength, so he jogged instead. Twenty minutes at a run, he had estimated. Twenty-five at this pace. Which would mean he would have to wait thirty minutes for medical assistance.

The calculations he was making were necessary and served as a distraction for mere seconds. When he looked down, Molly's hands had dropped from the back of her head to her face.

"Home," she murmured.

"Yes, my love. We're going home."

At that, her hands dropped, and her weight grew heavier. She had passed out. The damage done to her face was still unknown, because blood had run from the largest wound in many directions, confirming to him she had fought him off. The human died too fast, without pain. He wanted to go back and revive the bastard just so he could slice up his face, too. The anger he felt spurred him on, faster than before. He hadn't wanted to cause further damage, but at this rate, she would die in his arms, anyway. He stopped, only to hear her heart rate. It was fading. "No!"

His shoes pounded the pavement as he ran through the network of alleyways, and through his gate to the lake. When he laid her down, she was unresponsive. He ripped her shirt apart to see where she had been stabbed, then ripped off his so he could put pressure on her wound.

"Molly." Tears burned down his cheek. She was dying. If he gave her his blood now, she may not survive the transition. "Please," he pleaded, wanting to touch her face, but couldn't.

Air hitched in and out of her mouth, for she could not breathe through her nose, so he sucked in a gulp of oxygen and gave her mouth to mouth. Theodore placed his head on her chest to hear her heartbeat, but he heard nothing because the sound of a helicopter was in the distance. And it was coming in his direction.

Sebastian had his own helicopters, and as soon as Theodore rang him, he wasted no time. He flew over the roads that would have taken an hour or more to drive along and was about to land within the grounds of Theodore's home. He saw them by the lake, thankful that Theodore had chosen a spot in which he could easily land.

When he felt the ground beneath him, he jumped out, slid the side door open, and retrieved a stretcher and medical supplies. Theodore had Molly cradled in his arms, and when he looked at him as if he were a lifeline, he choked.

He was more than a council member; he had been a doctor since time began. A doctor, not a miracle worker. But for Theodore, he would do everything in his power. For Molly, his new friend and ally, he would perform a miracle.

"Help me put her on the stretcher in case we need to take her to a hospital." He could tell Theodore didn't want to let her go, so he gently peeled her from his arms. "Have you given her your blood?"

"No, she might die."

He put an oxygen mask on her and then put a pressure pack on her wound. "She'll die anyway, if you don't. If she's not too far gone, your blood will reconstruct her DNA and heal her. Do it now. Now!"

Sebastian saw Theodore's indecision before ripping open his wrist. He then moved the mask out of the way so the blood could drip into her mouth, then he replaced it.

"What now?" Theodore bellowed.

"I need to stop the bleeding. The injury is consistent with a stab wound. How long was the knife?"

"What? Just do something, will you?" His tone was urgent, frightened. "Help her."

Sebastian took control of the situation by speaking calmly. "The wound is right below her rib cage. I need to rule out a punctured lung."

"Three, four inches."

Enough to puncture the lung, he thought, *depending on the direction.* He checked the inside of her oxygen mask for signs of blood spots; if there were, it would mean her lungs were filling with fluid. There was blood. "Shit."

"What? What is it?"

"Wait. That's a cut on her lip, isn't it? Hold down the pressure pack." Sebastian pulled some gauze and a fresh oxygen mask out from his med bag, then ripped a piece of the cloth to cover the wound on her lip before putting the mask on.

After a few seconds, he inspected the mask. No blood spots. "Her lungs are fine. It's blood loss. Theodore, she needs blood. Get me some bags. She smells like a B-negative to me. Go. Now."

"I… I can't leave her." The anguish in Theodore's eyes was something Sebastian would remember for the rest of his life.

"Help me help her by getting the blood—now."

When Theodore sprinted to the house, he looked at Molly's battered face. "You will survive this. Do you understand?" He placed the backs of his fingers on her forehead and felt that her skin was on fire. She was transitioning at a much faster rate than expected. "No. I need more time."

"Theodore," he bellowed. "Hurry."

Chapter Nineteen

Molly thought she was trapped in a burning building while she travelled from the realm of dreams, only to wake up still on fire. The scream she heard was her own, and she knew this only because she felt it burn through her throat. "Theodore."

"I'm here. I'm here. Look at me."

Her eyes burned when she opened them, but she wanted to see him. She had to see him. "What's happening to me?"

Through her blurry vision, she saw he'd come closer. "I can't hear you. What did you say, Molly?"

"Keep her still and keep her talking," said a familiar voice. It was Sebastian's, she thought. Perhaps she hadn't woken up after all. She looked down, seeing that it was him. His movements were frantic over her midsection. Whatever it was he was doing to her, she didn't feel it over the scolding pain vibrating through her body.

"Molly, stay with me. Please, don't leave me." Theodore was nose to nose with her when he spoke.

A fresh wave of pain paralysed her when she tried to speak.

"She's not responding," he said to Sebastian. "What should I do?"

Sebastian spoke evenly. "Keep talking to her. Tell her where we are."

"We're home, by the lake."

Looking past his face, she saw the stars. She was by the lake. The water, she thought. The cool water. She raked her fingers through the grass, then steadied herself to roll over to her side.

"Keep her still. I have a couple more stitches to do."

"Water," she rasped. "Need. Cold."

"You want a glass of water?" Theodore said, sounding just as panicked as before when she could respond.

"She wants to cool herself down," Sebastian said. "We can't put her in the lake yet, she could go into shock. Cup the water in your hands and splash it over her face."

The ground vibrated beneath her when he ran to the lake. When he poured cool water over her face, the pain she was in subsided for a moment. "Water," she asked.

Again, he got some more, and then again. The third time, he poured it over her neck and chest.

"Theodore, pour the next one over her face. I want to see something," Sebastian said. There was a pause while he waited, then after Theodore did what he asked him to do, he said, "Look, there. Her cut is healing and her nose has straightened. Wait!" He moved Theodore out of the way so he could put his ear close to her face. "She's breathing through her nose."

"She's going to survive this, isn't she? Tell me she is going to survive this."

Regardless of what Sebastian said next, she would survive this. Because if she didn't, Theodore would die shortly after her. It would also mean that they wouldn't have the time they should have had.

Time had always been her enemy, either by going too slowly or too fast. Stealing moments of joy or keeping her suspended in times of sorrow. Time was something she had fought against her whole life and lost. For Theodore, she would win this round.

"She's still bleeding from this wound. Give me a few more minutes."

Wanting to let Theodore know she was going to pull through no matter what, she mustered as much strength as she could to speak a full sentence. "Have you fed Hallow yet?"

There was a laugh brought on by relief from both of them. "No, I haven't. You will do it yourself, okay? You will feed her, and then you will watch her sleep."

Molly tried to smile, but it took too much strength.

"The stitches I put in will have to come out now, before her skin heals over the top of them. Open your wrist again and let her drink. Then we can put her in the lake to cool her down."

"You said we couldn't. Is she going to survive this? I need to hear you say it."

“We can put her in the water now because she is going to survive this. She’s going to be fine in a matter of hours.”

When Theodore put his wrist over her mouth, blood trickled over her tongue, and her gums burned with the sweetest of all the pains—an itch-that-needed-to-be-scratched type of pain.

“Bite down on my wrist before my wound closes,” he instructed.

Before she complied, she ran her tongue over her teeth, finding that two were longer, sharper than the rest. She had done it, survived it.

* * *

Theodore cradled Molly in his arms while sitting in the shallow waters of the lake, looking up into each other’s eyes.

“How are you feeling now?” he said.

“My bones still feel like they’re smouldering, but they’re not as bad as they were.”

Sebastian spoke from the water’s edge. “You’re both very lucky. I don’t know of any human that would have survived transition after sustaining the injuries you did. We’ll have to document it.”

Theodore turned in his direction. “I could not have done this without you. I owe you a debt that could never be repaid.”

“I can think of a few things,” he teased. “I won’t ask what happened here tonight because you’ve both been through enough, but I hope the person paid for what they did to her.”

"They did," Theodore said.

"Good. I'll see you both next month."

At that, he left. Theodore put his hands over her ears before Sebastian started the helicopter's engine. Even so, the sound was deafening. As she watched it fly past, Theodore's face came back into view. His expression was of pure relief, softening his features. She wanted to touch his face, then she wanted to run her hand down his neck to his chest. Biting her now healed lip, she felt the painful burn turn into a more desirable one—passion. Thinking this was inappropriate, she went to grab her hair, only to remember she didn't have it anymore. Tears sprang from her eyes. "It's gone."

"What's gone, my love? Nothing has gone. You're going to be okay."

"My hair. It's gone."

Theodore shifted her in his lap. "This hair." He pulled a handful from behind her.

Molly grabbed it like a lifeline. "How?" Her once waist-length hair was to her shoulders. "Where's the rest of it?"

"It's growing at an accelerated rate. It will all be there in the next few hours. Don't worry."

"But how?"

"You're a vampire now. Healed, stronger, healthier."

She touched her face. "Will I have scars?"

"Your skin is unblemished, my love." He kissed her.

"How did you know I needed help? I wrote you a letter saying I would be back."

"The cameras. I almost left the room to get something when I saw you arrive and that the lights were on in your home." He paused, looking distressed. "What would have happened if I had left the room?"

"Let's not think about it. But how did you know from the lights… Oh, you knew about him, didn't you? From previous footage?"

"You feel betrayed, as is your right. However, you should know I would never have intruded into your life. You memorised me, and I was alone… I, umm…"

Molly placed her finger over his lips. "'Umm' is not a word. Theodore, all is forgiven. I wouldn't be here if not for you. I wouldn't be here to live this amazing life with you if not for your cameras. Let's put it behind us."

He nibbled her finger. "I believe I saw desire in your eyes before panic set in. Do you want me?"

"Yes."

"Now?" he said, kissing her neck.

"Yes. Now."

He laughed against her skin, sending vibrations through her body in the most delicious of ways. "When you're fully healed and your bones are no longer smouldering, I will make love to you until you fall asleep."

"No, now. I need this… you. I need you." She ripped open his shirt with ease, then frowned at her own strength. She was strong now, and even though he had her in a tight grip, she easily manoeuvred out of it, then straddled his waist. "Now."

He pulled her jumper up and over her head, then tore her bra at the centre as if it were made of paper before throwing it behind him.

When Theodore scraped his fangs over her nipple, she trembled in his arms. "Again," she said. When he did, she held his head in place. Never had she been so demanding. "Yes."

Needing to feel him inside her, she fumbled with the buttons of his jeans, feeling frustrated. Wanting what she wanted in equal measure, Theodore stood them both up so she could pull down his jeans while he ripped hers off. The sound of the material tearing heightened her desire. He spun her around until her back was to his chest. Then, like he had done before, he lowered her to her knees. Molly found his cock and positioned it for her pleasure before going onto her hands to steady herself.

"You want me inside you?"

"Yes. Now."

"My little vampire bride will be hungry for more than just blood."

"Theodore, please."

When he entered her, he stretched her in all the right places, making them both moan. As his thrusts became faster, the sound of the splashing water and the ripples in the lake mirrored her own build up. His fingers bit into her waist before he stilled her, then she felt his cock pulse when he came inside her—deep inside her, pushing her over the edge.

She was about to collapse fully into the water when Theodore caught her around her waist. He pulled her to his chest again, then turned her around so her legs were either side of his waist.

"Tell me how you are feeling now?" he murmured against her neck.

"Amazing. I feel amazing."

He responded to her by biting her neck. The sensation of it was like no other. It was sensual, sacred. Between them, it was love. Something they wouldn't have been able to share if she had remained a human. Something he would have sacrificed—for her.

She felt his cock hardened again, and rubbed herself against it. With one hand holding her head in place, he used the other to knead her bum before lifting her above his tip. As he entered her again, she came again.

"Again," she said.

"All night." He angled her head to his neck. "Feed from me, my love. Take what is yours."

* * *

Theodore hadn't told June what had happened yet. He had told Molly that everything had happened so fast and even after she had pulled through; he hadn't told her because he didn't want to worry her while Bill recovered and had also told Molly not to tell her about James until after Bill had settled.

When Molly had asked him about James, she didn't know he was dead. She had felt nothing after Theodore told her what he'd done and how Sebastian had dealt with the body; not sorrow or relief, just… nothing. Although, knowing he wouldn't be able to hurt anyone else was a plus for the world. Theodore had said she had nothing to worry about—and never would. And she believed him.

That was a couple of days ago now, and June and Bill were on their way back from the hospital.

"And they'll definitely come here before they go to their cottage," she asked, straightening the napkins next to the cake she'd made for them. It was strange, baking a cake she had no desire to eat. Even the aromas it gave off while it baked did nothing for her, and she knew why. Vampire or not, the only scent that could ever spark desire would be Theodore, her husband.

"They said they would. I can hear their car pulling up the driveway as we speak." He pulled her to him, nipping the tip of her ear.

She leaned into him, needing him again. "Don't start something we can't finish."

"Or, you could try exercising some control." He laughed, and she giggled.

"Would you really want that?"

"No, I wouldn't."

She unwound herself from his arms, then went over to reposition the napkins, wanting everything to be perfect for when they arrived. Life wasn't perfect, or rather, it hadn't been for her. Now that it was, she wanted to spread her joy—especially to June and Bill.

When Molly heard the front door open, Hallow followed her from the kitchen to greet them. As soon as June locked eyes with hers, she looked Molly up and down, then her chin trembled.

"You did it. It's done." June sounded relieved, tears of joy gathered in her eyes.

Theodore had explained to her what June had done and why she had done it in more detail, making Molly love her even more.

"Come here," June said, opening up her arms to embrace Molly.

Bill used his crutches to step closer to her. "You look even more beautiful than before, if that's at all possible. I'll put it down to you being in love, rather than you being a vampire. If that's okay with you?"

Molly cocked her head, trying to figure out what he meant by that. "Yeah, that's okay."

He smiled. "Seeing is believing, but I'm incapable of accepting the truth, I'm afraid. My mind just won't allow it."

"Theodore said it took you twenty years before you accepted what he was. It's okay. I still have a lot to learn, and I'm sure there will be parts of it I will have a hard time believing."

"Like the garden gnomes?"

Molly looked at Theodore, searching for the truth. Surely not. He smiled wide, fangs on display. "He's teasing you."

"Oh, ha. Not funny, Bill." She covered her face with her hands.

"Come here and give me a hug," he said, passing his crutches to June. After he squeezed Molly in his arms, he said, "I'm told you have a surprise for me."

"I do. It's in the kitchen."

While she chatted with Bill on the way, she heard June ask Theodore where the gate was.

"I'll tell you everything when you and Bill have settled. That being said, I will need you to take care of something while we're away," he said.

Molly turned. "We're going away. Where? What does June need to take care of?"

He grinned. "June will need a new assistant because the last one got fired for breaking all of my house rules. And someone is coming in for an interview while we are in Paris."

Molly stood, stunned. "I got fired? We're going to Paris?"

He ran his fingers through her hair. "I want to see your artwork in the most prestigious galleries in the world, where they belong." He kissed her hand. "Tell me, my love. How does it feel now you are a full-time artist?"

The End.

ABOUT THE AUTHOR

Kelly Barker was born in Oxford and now lives in Witney with her husband and dog, Lana. She has been a barber for over twenty years, and loves her job. However, reading and writing is her passion—a passion handed down to her by her great grandmother, Isobel O'Leary.

www.kellybarker.org

Sleep-deprived Zoe lives in her own imagination, struggling between home and work life as a barber… finding it easier each day to slip into a world that doesn't exist. Or does it?

Hell bent on completing a story she is writing to right a wrong, she unknowingly creates a storyline so powerful, it gives the main character Ivy—a vampire queen—the means to escape off the pages and into the real world.

To secure her freedom, Ivy must destroy the writer. However, Zoe doesn't know what's real or what her mind has conjured. Is this a part of her overactive imagination? Or can she accept her gift, using it to send Ivy back within the pages?

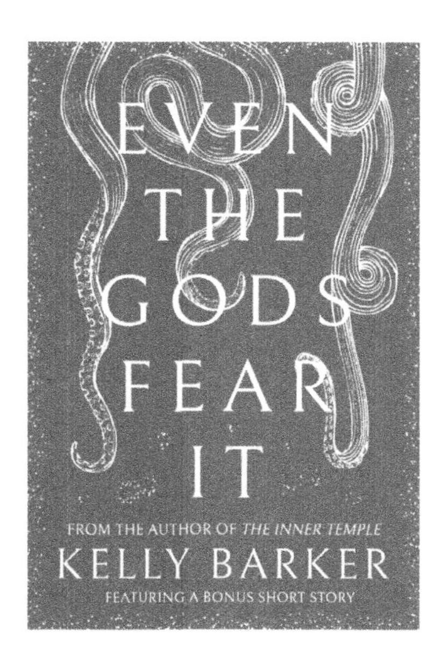

Zoe is torn between her newfound abilities to create characters into existence through her storytelling and her loved ones. Her fiance Bowen wants to protect her, but she feels as though she can't breathe.

When Bowen sets sail, taking one last trip to save the plesiosaurs from extinction, she and Varik, one of her creations, release something so deadly it's rumoured that even the gods fear it.

She is now faced with two choices. With the world divided over her creations, the line between right and wrong has become blurred. Will Zoe finally understand that you can't have all that power without repercussions? Or will she lose everything?

Cokehead Max comes from a long line of spiritualists. With each generation becoming more powerful than the last to fulfil a prophecy bestowed upon them.

When Max's grandma dies, not only is he forced into a world he wants no part of, he has to pay his grandma's debt for violating the rules governed by Ebony – the guardian of the realm between life and death.

Can Max's family—divided by secrecy and grief—unite to defeat both the prophecy and the seemingly rogue guardian? Or is it too late?

www.kellybarker.org

'Served cold' is included in *Thanksgiving horror anthology.* Available from Amazon, Pubshare, Google Play, Apple Books, Nook, Kobo and Kindle.

Printed in Great Britain
by Amazon